Holding Pattern

ALSO BY JEFFERY RENARD ALLEN

FICTION
Rails Under My Back

POETRY
Harbors and Spirits
Stellar Places

Holding Pattern

JEFFERY RENARD ALLEN

Jeffery Lenard Allen

Stories

Graywolf Press
SAINT PAUL, MINNESOTA

Copyright © 2008 by Jeffery Renard Allen

Publication of this volume is made possible in part by a grant provided by the Minnesota State Arts Board, through an appropriation by the Minnesota State Legislature; a grant from the Wells Fargo Foundation Minnesota; and a grant from the National Endowment for the Arts, which believes that a great nation deserves great art. Significant support has also been provided by the Bush Foundation; Target; the McKnight Foundation; and other generous contributions from foundations, corporations, and individuals. To these organizations and individuals we offer our heartfelt thanks.

Special funding for this title has been provided by the Jerome Foundation.

The stories in this collection first appeared in other publications: "Bread and the Land" in *Antioch Review*; "It Shall Be Again" in *African Voices*, reprinted in *110 Stories: New York Writes After September 11*, edited by Ulrich Baer, New York University Press; "Shimmy" in *Other Voices*; "Toilet Training" in *Antioch Review*; "Holding Pattern" in *Literary Review*; "Mississippi Story" in *Story Quarterly*; "Dog Tags" in *Bomb*; "Same" in *Land-Grant College Review*; "The Green Apocalypse" in *Other Voices*; "The Near Remote" in *Chicago Noir*, edited by Neal Pollack, Akashic Books.

Published by Graywolf Press
2402 University Avenue, Suite 203
Saint Paul, Minnesota 55114
All rights reserved.

www.graywolfpress.org

Published in the United States of America

ISBN 978-1-55597-509-8

2 4 6 8 9 7 5 3 1
First Graywolf Printing, 2008

Library of Congress Control Number: 2008928246

Cover design: Kapo Ng@A-Men Project

for
Elijah, Jewel, and Sophia—heart of my heart

Special thanks to the Whiting Foundation, Creative Capital, and the Dorothy and Lewis B. Cullman Center for Scholars and Writers at the New York Public Library for their generous support

The land may be spoiled, yet it will remain intact.
– DINKA PROVERB

Contents

Note: Though the name Hatch appears in many of the stories that follow, the reader should not assume that this name represents a single, reappearing character.

Holding Pattern

Bread and the Land

I hear my train a comin.
— JIMI HENDRIX

Black flutter, Mamma flashed about the room, workbound, her shiny knee-length black leather boots working against the wood floor like powerful pistons. Up, down, up, down. She stopped and looked at the space around her. I have everything, she said. The hem ends of her long black dress flared like wings.

Yes, you do, Hatch said. He waited patiently on the bed edge, warm, his snowsuit packing him tight in heat and sweat, all of him sausaged inside puffy outer skin.

She put herself before a full-length mirror, flexed a black hat onto her plump head, and slipped inside a black fur coat. The hat was real fur, but the coat, some imitation material.

You look dashing, he said.

Thank you.

He watched her with hot pride. She was heavyset but pretty. Even with her second chin, she was ten times prettier than the mother of any classmate at school.

The phone rang on the faded brass nightstand next to the bed. Uh. Who could that be? People always call you at the wrong time. She lifted the receiver to her ear. Hello. Her eyes widened. It's Blunt, she said.

3

Oh, he said. My grandmother. He didn't like his grandmother.

You must go to work, he said. Tell her. Be frank.

Words chirped in the earpiece. Mamma brightened. The preacher's dead, she said.

Oh, he said.

The preacher's dead.

That's good, he said.

She gave him a hard look. Placed her hand over the mouthpiece. Don't get smart.

He didn't say anything.

Put those things in Mamma's bag, she said.

A small duffel bag lay unopened on the bed.

Okay, he said. He picked up her rubber gloves, pulled the fingers, and let them snap.

She looked at him. You know not to make noise when I'm on the phone.

Fine. He crammed the gloves, a white smock, white rubber-soled shoes, deodorant, and a bar of soap into the bag, which spread at the sides, stuffed like a holiday turkey.

Yes, Blunt, Mamma said. Okay, Blunt. I understand.

Blunt and the preacher lived in New York City, in Harlem, point of origin for a nationwide chain of funeral homes. Just around the corner from where Hatch lived, a Progressive Funeral Home entombed an entire street, the name spelled out in square orange blocks lit from inside, like supermarket letters. A man-high wrought-iron fence surrounded and secured the parking lot, four redbrick columns for corners, each topped with a white globe at the end of a long stem-slim black metal pole.

Blunt and the preacher own that, Mamma liked to say.

Yes, Blunt. My grandmother.

Snooping, he had found two other Progressive Funeral Homes listed in the local telephone directory.

Name and deed, Blunt traveled through his mind like some inky

JEFFERY RENARD ALLEN

substance. He had never spied photograph the first—Mamma had burned all existing images many years before he was born—or heard her voice. Once a month, Mamma mailed Blunt a letter with his most recent portrait, and Blunt mailed her a letter—typed, always typed—with a check.

Why doesn't Blunt send us more money?

She sends all she can.

How much is that?

Whatever she sends.

Fine.

Good-bye, Blunt, Mamma said. She hung up the phone. Turned to Hatch. Smiled. Hatch, come here.

What? he said.

Come over here to Mamma.

Is this something frank?

Yes.

What?

Blunt's coming to live with us.

Nawl.

Don't use that street language.

I'm not.

Choose your words carefully.

Who's coming to live with us?

Blunt.

My grandmother?

Yes.

Why is she coming to live with us?

Because the preacher's dead.

So?

The preacher's dead, so now she can come live with us.

How come she didn't come live with us when the preacher was alive?

You know why.

No, I don't.

Don't talk back. And don't talk countrified.

How come she never visited us?

You know why.

I don't know why. Tell me. Be frank. Good people are always frank.

I am being frank.

You ain't.

Watch your language and stop talking back.

I ain't talkin back.

Mind your mouth.

How did the preacher die?

Suddenly.

Oh.

You know that the preacher had a bad heart.

Who had a bad heart?

Be a good boy for Mamma.

I am being good.

Then we'll let Blunt stay in your room when she comes.

Nawl. I don't want her around me. He liked his small room, high above the world, a third-story nest to which he flew for refuge.

We're going to move your things into my room so that Blunt can put her things in your room.

Nawl.

It'll only be for a little while. Blunt has lots of money now, and she wants to buy us a house, and we'll all live together, and you'll have a big room.

She lyin.

Watch your mouth. You get worse every day.

I do not.

And stop talking back.

He said nothing.

You can sleep in my room when she comes.

Nawl. I'll sleep in the kitchen *if* she comes.

What did I tell you about talking back?

I'm not talking back.

She *is* coming.

Fine.

Okay?

Fine.

You'll be a good boy for Mamma when she comes?

Fine.

She knows how smart you are.

Fine.

The train screeched around the curve, the passengers firm and erect in their seats like eggs in a carton. Hatch checked flight conditions. The El was a strong, sprawling nest erected over the city. Safe, Mamma beside him, he looked down on the world far below. Wormlike people wiggled through snow. Habit, they often rode like this, all day on Sundays. Mamma wanted him to memorize every route. He would touch the map like his skin.

Car to car, the train pulled into the station, a flock of magnetic migratory birds. They quit the bright metal insides and, hand in hand, pushed through the rushing crowd. His snowsuited legs rubbed together and made a noise like that of an emery board against fingernails. He kept his eyes low, sighting varied shoes and boots flopping like fish across the wet concrete floor, his blind forehead colliding with belted or fitted waists. His sight lifted to bright lights perched, pigeonlike, in the high conical roof.

Some fabled creature waited near the checkpoint to gate 12. Human, beast, and fowl. Feathery white mink hat and coat, red amphibian jumpsuit (leather? plastic?), and knee-length alligator boots. She was tall and wide like a man, and carried a white suitcase in one hand, a black guitar case in the other.

Mamma swallowed. That's Blunt, she said.

The creature called Blunt spotted Mamma and strode forward without hesitation, strode full of life. She halted two feet shy of them and set down the suitcase and the guitar case with equal care. Extended her hand. It was big. Mamma took the big hand into her own.

Hello, Joy, Blunt said.

Hello, Blunt, Mamma said.

Blunt released Mamma's hand. Seemed to think twice about it and gave Mamma a quick peck on the cheek. Studied Hatch. So this is my little Hatch, she said.

He studied her back. She was butt ugly. A net of wrinkles drew her skin tight. Her dark face masklike, coated with rouge. A flat pug nose some fist had mashed in. And long protruding jaws and lips, like a stork's mouth. Nothing baby about her face. Nothing. Thinking this, he was forced to admit that she had pretty eyes. Green.

Come give your granny a hug, she said. Spread her arms wide. He didn't move. She bent down and hugged him tight, forcing his constricted lungs to breathe in her perfume. Strawberry pop. He didn't like strawberry pop.

She released him and rose back to her full height.

Where's your other suitcases? he asked. Mamma pinched him. She only pinched; she would never strike him. She'd had two still-births; he was her only child.

What? Blunt asked.

Where's your other suitcases? Mamma pinched him again. If you're coming to live with us, then where's your other suitcases? You can't put nothing in no one suitcase.

Blunt gave him a fierce cold look, eyelashes so stiff with mascara, they resembled tiny claws. Now, you're a smart little boy, so you know I'm having the rest of my things shipped.

I don't know nothing.

Mamma looked at him, hard. Blunt green-watched him. Such a pity. You look so cute in that snowsuit.

They left the station for the taxi stand. A storm had set in; snow sprayed his face, white, wet, and cold. Blunt walked over to the lead cab, a fat yellow block, and roused the driver, a short man with short thick legs.

How you today, ma'am?

Just fine, Blunt said.

The driver placed her white suitcase inside the yellow trunk.

She opened the passenger door, slid the guitar case on the floor, then held the door wide. Mamma motioned for Hatch to get in. He did. She followed. Blunt held her hat with one hand, ducked inside the cab, and seated herself. Mamma hadn't held her own hat. Blunt shut the door. The motor roared to life. The driver slammed the taxi into gear. Where to?

Mamma told him.

Enjoy your ride.

They rode to the dull hum of the busy engine, the heat full blast, Hatch damp, his body boiling inside the meaty snowsuit. He studied Blunt's reflection in the driver's rearview mirror. She sat very stiff, green eyes staring straight ahead. Glad that he didn't have to sit next to her.

Easy motion and casual heat, they cruised in bubbled metal. No one moved. No one spoke. Three monkeys, deaf, mute, and blind. They rode on past Hatch's school, Andrew Carnegie Elementary. Mamma gestured to Blunt. Blunt nodded and smiled. Traffic started to thicken. The driver took cautionary measures, dodging around the El's pylons, only to get pinned between a pylon and some stalled cars.

Move this thing, sir, Blunt said.

I'm doin all I can, ma'am.

Well, move it.

I'm sure we'll be moving soon, Blunt, Mamma said.

Look, I'm paying you good money! Blunt watched the driver with her green eyes.

This will go much better if we all jus relax, the driver said.

Hatch peered through the frosty cab window. Thickly clothed people hurried by with their heads tucked against slanting wind and snow. Sheltered inside a doorway, a musician vied for attention. He was seated on a footstool, acoustic guitar angled across his body, strumming the strings and tapping an athletic shoed foot, an empty coffee can a few feet in front of him. His voice rose above snarling traffic and honking horns.

> If you don't wanna get down wit me
> You can't sit under my apple tree
> Say, if you don't wanna get—

One passerby tossed him a coin. Hatch felt all twisted inside. He caught Blunt's face in the rearview mirror. She too was watching the musician, effort in her looking. All the anger seemed to have left her. She saw Hatch seeing her and gave him an icy look.

She faced the driver. Driver, get this cab moving, she said.

He did, foot on the accelerator to race down lost time. The Progressive Funeral Home soon blinked by. Against Hatch's expectations, both Mamma and Blunt sat oblivious. He grunted. That Blunt! She ain't look at it cause she don't want me to know she ain't nothin but a phony.

They braked to a quick stop, bodies thrown forward and back. Blunt pulled rolled bills from a jumpsuit pocket, unfolded them, and licked her thumb and forefinger to catch the crispy edges. She paid the driver and tipped him five dollars. You don't deserve a tip, she said.

He smiled. Thanks anyway, ma'am. I'm gon get yo suitcase from the trunk.

Mamma frowned at his vocabulary.

Only if you're capable, Blunt said.

He's using that countrified language, Hatch said. The driver shot Hatch a glance. Mamma pinched him. But he speakin street. Mamma pinched him again. Stung, Hatch's arm was hot and hurt in the snowsuit. Hand on the door handle, he tried to make a quick exit. The door refused to budge. Frozen, perhaps. Blunt leaned across Mamma and opened it. She smiled. Hatch gave her a mean look.

They quit the cab, snow crunching underfoot. The short driver hoisted the suitcase from the trunk while Blunt pulled the guitar case from the floor.

All y'all have a nice day, the driver said. He shot Hatch another glance and grinned.

Mamma shook her head at the diction. Hatch gave the driver his meanest look.

Blunt passed the driver another five-dollar bill. Learn how to drive, she said.

Yes, ma'am. Thank you. He got inside the cab and sped off.

Three flights of stairs spiraled a challenge to the apartment above. Mamma started up, Blunt following—the suitcase in one hand, the guitar case in the other—and Hatch following her. At the top landing, Mamma leaned her tired weight on the banister, sucking for air. Seem like the *fourth* floor, she said. Blunt said nothing. Chest rising slow and easy. Hatch believed himself an excellent judge of age and had concluded that Blunt was *very* old—she was so ugly—but, having witnessed her feat on the stairs, he was now uncertain.

You got a nice apartment, Joy. She looked the kitchen over with her green eyes.

Thank you, Blunt. It's small but comfortable.

Well, don't you worry about that.

Mamma smiled.

Would you like some breakfast?

I sure would. Where do you keep your pans?

No. You must be tired from your trip. She lowered her eyes. Do you eat meat?

Blunt looked Mamma full in the face. Yes, Joy.

Well, let me show you to your room.

My room, Hatch thought. He was shaking, either from cold or heat—he couldn't tell—his arm still hot from the pinch.

Mamma looked at him. Go into the bathroom and get out of that snowsuit. She and Blunt started for Hatch's room. He watched them.

Joy, let Hatch keep me company. Blunt stopped her body like a truck and waited for a response.

Mamma didn't say anything for a moment. She turned and looked at Hatch. Hatch, hurry out of that snowsuit and come keep Blunt company.

Hatch watched Blunt, hard. Wind and snow had smeared the makeup around her eyes, the talon streaks of some huge bird.

Mamma came forward and gripped his hand. Be good, she whispered. Don't be mean and selfish like your father. She had been frank about his father. Normally, these words about his bad father would have settled him. He struggled to free his hand.

Be good, Mamma said.

He knew she would not hit him. No matter how angry she became. Mind working, he stared through the distance at Blunt. Formed a plan. He would pretend he liked Blunt. Alone with her, he would give her a piece of his mind. Choice words. All right, he said.

Mamma gave him a hard look that said, *Be good.* She pushed open one of the French doors that separated her room from his, then headed for the kitchen.

Hello, Hatch, Blunt said.

Hello, Blunt.

Blunt removed her coat and hung it in the closet. Her arms were thick inside the sleeves of the red jumpsuit. She removed her hat before the dresser mirror, intent on her reflection. Hair spilled gray and long about her shoulders. With her back to him, she began

JEFFERY RENARD ALLEN

unpacking the one suitcase, now open on the bed. She turned and smiled. Hummed low deep waters in her throat. *You can't fool me,* he thought. Puffy in his snowsuit, he watched her unpack and searched for the correct way to phrase what he wanted to say.

I mean, all that happened twenty-five, thirty, years ago. Blunt chased him out of town with her straight razor. Red, they called him, though I never saw him myself. Clay colored. Bowlegged. A midget. A bad man. Like your father.

Blunt kept his ten-dollar Sears Roebuck guitar and taught herself how to play it.

Then Blunt married the preacher-mortician. I was ten by this time. They'd known each other all along. We moved into his funeral home. It was like a castle, enough rooms to sleep fifty people. Plenty places to wander and get lost.

The preacher always spoke his mind. Children make me nervous. This is what he said. I got a bad heart, and people like me, with bad hearts, also have bad nerves, if you see my meaning. I did. So I kept fifteen feet away from him. Fifteen feet. Measured it.

He was the most disliked colored man in the Rains County. He kept a stable full of horses he had never learned to ride. (His bad heart.) And he had dainty ways like white folks. Always wore a suit and tie in the blazing heat, and walked with his head up high, and breathed like a rusty well pump, and sweated like a fountain. He would place his napkin in his lap when he ate and sweat down into it. He had been in a car accident that scarred up his face pretty bad. (You should have seen it. Unbelievable.) And he never ate meat, since it aggravated his scars. This is what he said: God saw to it to give me the accident, and with it, scars and a bad heart.

The accident had given him the calling to be a preacher, but his sermons put people to sleep. (Christ is fire and water insurance!) That was what led him into the mortuary business. Preachers must eat. He was the picture of success. (They often wrote him up in the newspapers.) With the dead in your corner, you can't fail. Not that he didn't have his problems. Rumor had it that he disrespected bodies placed in his care. (I never saw him myself.) He carved tic-tac-toe on skin. He stuffed hollow cavities with marbles. He drained insides with a garden hose. He embalmed with shoe polish. These accusations turned away no customers. He was cheap and allowed payment by installments and gave a free vase of flowers to the family of the deceased and guaranteed his caskets to resist rust and rot for fifty years.

Then this man—his name always escapes me—took things one step further. I was sixteen. One Sunday he entered the chapel shouting and screaming and cursing and woke the snoring congregation. He voiced his charges: The preacher had removed his wife's neck and put a short log in its place. And the preacher had wrapped that log in a pretty pink scarf to hide the evil deed. (I did see the scarf.) He pointed a sharp finger at the preacher. Your tail is mine, he said. And I got something fo that hefty woman of yours too.

The preacher's nerves took over after that. He would not let Blunt leave the house. And when he went out into the street, he took me along with him as his eyes and ears. He would look in every direction at once, scars twitching. Then he would put one hand over his heart, desperate to calm it. But the hand would jump every few seconds, like it had been given an electrical jolt. Then the wheezing would start, and I would guide him back to the parlor. This went on for about a week; then he and Blunt grabbed their hats and coats in the middle of the night and caught the first thing smoking.

I heard what you did, Hatch said. I know what you did. Mamma had always told him to respect adults, to speak when spoken to, but Blunt deserved no respect.

She stopped what she was doing and turned to him with her green eyes and wild mascara. Her big shoulders tense and her big hands stiff. What did you hear?

You know.

You tell me.

No, you tell me. Why did you do it? Why? Speak up. Be frank.

She studied him for a moment. Sometimes it just bees that way.

Fine, he said. Neither understanding nor caring to understand, he freed himself from the snowsuit and went into the kitchen, where Mamma was.

Were you good? she asked.

Yes.

Then why are you frowning?

I don't know.

You'll have to try harder to be good.

Fine.

Okay.

Fine.

A burly foreigner under an ugly red hat explains to a primly dressed man behind a desk why he wants a Liberty Express card: In our country, it is forbidden to wear fur hats or ride speedboats. The white man issues him the card. He zooms offscreen in a long red speedboat. The camera zooms in on the ugly red hat, buoyant on the water. Bubbles carry it under.

How many times had he seen that commercial over the day's slow course? They had sat in continual silence, no catching up on lost time, no planning for the found future. Mute monkeys.

Joy, why don't I prepare dinner?

No, don't trouble yourself. I'll do it.

Why don't we both do it? Blunt smiled.

You don't have to.

It'll be fun. We'll do it together.

I would like that, Mamma said. But why don't I cook and you stay here with Hatch and let Hatch keep you company?

Blunt hesitated. That's a good idea.

Mamma went into the kitchen. Blunt and Hatch watched the television.

Quiet day, Blunt said.

Yes.

Shadow and light, her face flickered. What's yo favorite show?

The Phony from Harlem.

They sat around the round wood kitchen table, with platters of fried chicken, black-eyed peas, corn bread, and candied yams in easy reach. They sat like quiet spectators, as if waiting for the food to perform. A roach crawled onto the table.

Mamma forced a chuckle. These roaches are about to run us out of here, she said.

Blunt smashed the roach with her hand, as swift as a judge's gavel. Mamma turned her eyes away. Stunned like the roach, Hatch watched Blunt until she rose to wash her nasty hand.

Mamma cleared the table. All three moved into the living room, before the TV, and sat down, not saying anything. Blunt faced Hatch, some half-formed song in her wide throat.

He watched her. When you gon play that guitar? he asked. Blunt was a phony, and he would prove it.

Hatch! Mamma said.

Joy, it's okay. She looked at Hatch. Why don't you bring it to me?

Disbelieving, he rushed over to the guitar—invisible inside its armored case—tensed, stooped down, and lifted it. It was light, weightless. He brought it over and set it down at Blunt's feet. Blunt shifted forward in her seat, crouched over the case, flipped open the latches, and removed the guitar. Clean bright color. Sun and flame. And thick, cablelike strings that hovered an inch above the finger-board and the sound hole (a deep dark cave). *I bet that's Red's old guitar*, Hatch thought. *Too cheap to buy a new one.*

Blunt plucked the strings with her right thumb—big as a shoehorn—while she twisted the tuning pegs with her left fingers, releasing long scraping vibrations like those of a dragging muffler. Hands working, she tested the strings some more and nodded to herself when she achieved the desired pitch.

And now, for my next tune—

Hatch did not laugh at her joke.

She cleared her throat. Stroked the strings and set them humming. Opened her mouth wide in song.

> *Sweet daddy, bring back yo sweet jelly roll*
> *Sweet daddy, bring back yo sweet jelly roll*
> *Don't leave me this way*
> *Burdened with this heavy load*

Hatch's heart tightened. He rode deep waves of thought and feeling that carried him to some far-off place in the room, where he sat alone, in a small boat, spiraling on a whirlpool of blue water.

Mamma started briskly for the kitchen. Hatch went dizzily after her. Mamma? Where you going?

To do my cleaning.

Come and hear Blunt.

I can hear her from in here.

Come hear. A lasting spray of blue water, cool on his skin.

Come see Blunt play.

You go back and watch her.

He went back. Why you stop? Go on. Play some more.

No. It's late in the evening. Folks trying to sleep. Blunt put the guitar back inside the case and closed lid and latches. Maybe I'll teach *you* how to play tomorrow.

Really?

Yes.

I'd like that.

Mamma came into the room. Hatch, bedtime.

Fine.

Time for bed.

Fine.

Good night, Mamma said. She kissed him.

Good night.

Good night, Blunt said. She kissed him, her big lips wet on his face, her pug nose hard against his cheek.

Good night. Anger dragged him from the room and to a dark thinking place under Mamma's bedsheets.

He lay there for some time, weighing, calculating, then quietly left the bed at the precise moment when Mamma and Blunt would falsely believe him asleep. He tiptoed over to the French doors and put his ear to the cold squared glass.

Please try.

I will.

You know plenty. So please . . .

I understand.

Yes. That's all I'm asking. He's still young.

I will.

Well, I said my piece. Good night, Blunt.

Good night, Joy . . . daughter.

Hatch hurried back into bed and pulled the covers over his head. He heard Mamma enter the room. Felt the opposite side of the mattress sag under her weight. He kept his back toward her as a wall and waited for sleep to come.

I must leave for work.

Why? Blunt said. I see no need.

Mamma seemed to ponder the words. Thank you, Blunt. I'm glad to hear you say that.

No need to thank me. Those bones is tired. It's time for some rest.

I won't argue . . . Well, I better get Hatch to school.

You two go ahead. I'll stay here and get some rest. Still ain't got that train out of my system.

Okay, Mamma said.

Good-bye, Blunt, Hatch said. He smiled up at her.

Good-bye, Hatch. Yall need money for a cab? It's a bad day out there.

That would be nice, Mamma said.

Rubber boots inches above the floor, Hatch floated on the seat, an astronaut in his inflated snowsuit.

Why do I have to go to school today?

Because that's your responsibility.

You got frank with me about Blunt and the preacher and you got frank with me about my father because you want me to be responsible? She had once explained it to him.

Yes.

Is Blunt responsible?

Why do you ask?

She still be responsible if she run away from the preacher?

Good people stick by those who are good to them.

The preacher was good?

Yes.

That's not what you said.

What did I say?

You know what you said.

You misunderstood.

He was good?

Yes?

Why?

He helped her.

Are you being frank?

Yes.

They swung over to the curb.

Be good. She kissed his cheek.

I will. He wasn't sure if she had been frank.

She paid the driver. Driver, could you please wait? I'll be right back.

You got it.

They quit the cab and took the short path to the school.

Be good.

I will.

When school let out, he found Mamma waiting for him in an idling cab. He spoke excitedly about a typical school day. They had a quick ride home, the cab seemingly sliding above the snow like a great yellow sled.

Blunt! Blunt! We're home!

He ran freely through the apartment. Blunt's eyes stopped him, heavy on mind and skin, holding him in place like paperweights.

What happened to your eyes? Hatch asked. They're blue.

I'll show you. Blunt moved into Hatch's bedroom, her large body in blue silk pajamas, hair flowing like a silver wave down to her nape. She returned with a small plastic case resting on her palm. These are contact lenses, she said.

What? Hatch said.

She removed something from the case, raised her hand to her eye. Removed her hand. Now her eye was green. The other was still blue.

How'd you do that?

Contact lenses, she said. She held out the case, full of many colored lenses, painted Easter eggs.

Wow.

Those are lovely, Mamma said.

Blunt smiled with radiant satisfaction. Eager to please, she turned her eye gray, then light brown, then green, then blue again.

Lahzonyah, Blunt called it. Lah-zon-yah. He tried to rise to his feet but found himself anchored to the seat, his stomach heavy with sunken treasure, the long empty casserole dish abandoned in the middle of the table like a beached boat.

Play some music.

Mamma glared at him over the hot coffee at her lips.

Maybe later, Hatch. Let my food digest first.

How long will that take?

Blunt laughed. Do you know that I used to have my own place where I could play music anytime I wanted and where dozens and dozens of people would come see me?

Mamma noisily returned her cup to the saucer.

What did you call it? Hatch asked.

The Red Rooster.

Did it look like a red rooster?

Blunt laughed. No. Like a barn. The only barn in Harlem.

Did it have—

Saturday, we should do some sightseeing, Mamma said. The coffee steamed up into her face. You haven't seen the city.

That'll be fine, Blunt said. How does that sound to you, Hatch?

Fine, he said. Please play your guitar tonight.

Why don't you ask your mother if it's okay with her?

Hatch looked at Mamma.

She was a long time in answering. I don't see why not.

Great. Blunt hammered a beat on the table with her roach-slaying palm.

After some time, she arranged herself in a chair with her guitar.

> *If you gon walk on my heart*
> *Please take off yo shoes*
> *Said, if you gon walk on my heart*
> *Kindly take off yo shoes*
> *I got miles to make up to you, baby*
> *And I ain't got no time to lose*

Bright stringed music radiated from the sunburst guitar and enwebbed the entire room. Job done, the rays recoiled back into the dark sound hole.

Play another one!

Bedtime, Mamma said.

No, it's not.

Bedtime.

It's too early.

Bedtime.

Fine.

Come on.

Fine.

Good night, Hatch. Blunt kissed him.

Good night.

He stalked out of the room. Pounced upon Mamma's bed and clawed the sheets. Voices on the other side of the glassed door tamed his anger.

I asked you.

I'm sorry.

I mean—

I really am sorry.

I explained my reasons.

Yes. He is a child.

I mean, you know plenty. What was that one the preacher liked?

"Unchanging Hand."

Yes. How about that one?

A solid choice.

I've tried. Tried my best. I've been patient. More than patient. I'm not one to cry over spoiled milk.

No, you aren't. And bless you for it. If you put spoiled milk in the refrigerator at night, it'll still be spoiled in the morning.

Yes.

Oh, Joy, I know. You may not believe it, but I know. You see,

I ain't much to look at. No feast for the eye. But the preacher chose me.

He wasn't a pretty man himself.

No, he wasn't, but he was a good man . . . Sometimes you had to fish for it. And good fish stay deep. Only the dead ones float on top.

Well, Mamma said, one might look at it that way.

Spoiled milk and dead fish both stink.

That's true.

Good night, Joy. Daughter.

Good night, Blunt. Mother.

The next morning Hatch rose early and watched Mamma wake from the gray paralysis of sleep. She struggled out of bed, her hands positioned at her chest like a gloved surgeon's, careful not to touch anything or let anything touch her. More than once he had watched her sore hands soak for hours in a deep tub of warm water and Epsom salt.

Mamma?

What?

Is Blunt sad?

What makes you think that?

Is she sad because the preacher died?

I don't know.

Is that why she can sing and stroke and make—

Don't talk that way.

I'm being frank.

You aren't being frank. Don't talk like that.

How come she likes to—

That's enough. Get ready for school.

They bathed and clothed themselves, then entered the kitchen, the table set and breakfast prepared. Blunt followed her sweet heavy perfume into the room, tight leather jumpsuit and tall leather boots slowing and constricting her movement, and her makeup so thick, she struggled to keep her chin up.

Good morning, Blunt.

Good morning, Joy.

Good morning, Hatch.

Good morning, Blunt. Blunt bent down—her eyes gray—and kissed him, then drew herself straight. In that space of time he glimpsed something in her face.

They all sat down at the round wood table.

Why are you dressed so early? Mamma asked.

I'm going out to buy some new guitar strings.

Mamma didn't say anything.

Maybe I'll even buy a new guitar.

Can you find your way around?

Sure. I'll take a cab.

Mamma, let Blunt take me to school today.

Remember your place.

No, Joy. It's okay.

No, it's not okay. He's too smart for his own good.

That is so. How bout I take him to school today—if it's okay with you.

Mamma hesitated. Looked at Blunt. Looked at Hatch. Looked at Blunt again. Perhaps that would be good.

Blunt smiled.

I'll write down the address. Just show it to the driver.

Of course.

Blunt sat next to him, like a big block of ice in her white fur coat. The weather had not changed. For the first time, he was glad to be inside the padded snowsuit. Kind. The two of them all plump, like fresh pastries on display. But he found it hard to keep still in his seat, victim to the stab of wondering. Should he confront her about what he thought he'd glimpsed in her eyes? Confront her about what he'd overheard last night? Something about dead fish, spoiled milk, and funky smells. *Maybe she is a phony. Maybe she jus playin and singin to make me like her.* His curiosity caused him to sight down the guitar's polished neck, fret by fret—railroad ties—to the ragged paper edge of a brown grocery bag; and to continue down the bag's side, to a bottom corner and Blunt's black boot wedging it in place. Why had she not brought the case along? Surely Mamma had noticed. Should he—

How do you like school?

Just fine.

Of course you like it. You're a smart boy, and you're doing so well. I'm proud of you.

Thank you.

I was real proud when you graduated from kindergarten.

Hatch said nothing.

That beautiful picture Joy sent me.

Yes.

And now we're all together.

Yes.

I'll buy that new guitar and play something nice for you this evening.

Fine. Will you play—

Maybe. Let's wait and see what your mother wants to hear.

Why did you put yo guitar in that bag?

Blunt didn't say anything for a moment. Why, didn't I jus tell you? I plan to sell it.

Why you leave yo case at home?

I don't need it.

Why you ain't jus throw yo guitar away?

Some people are needy.

You want to help the needy people?

Yes.

So you want needy people to have yo guitar?

Yes.

Why?

Because—

Let me have it.

Oh. You don't want this old thing.

Why not?

It barely plays.

I thought you said you gon teach me how to play.

Yes.

Then I can use that old thing.

I'll buy you a nice new one.

Fine.

But—

Fine.

Wouldn't you like a new guitar?

Sure, he said. *But you ain't gon buy it*, he thought.

Enjoy school, Blunt said. She kissed him on the cheek.

I will, he said. Her pug nose looked like a big beetle stuck on to her face.

Good-bye, Hatch.

Good-bye, Blunt.

Where's Blunt?

Plumed exhaust rose from the idling cab.

She hasn't returned. Mamma spoke from the dark cavelike inside.

She was sposed to pick me up.

Mamma blinked nervously. Did she say that?

No.

Well.

I thought she was gon pick me up.

Watch your mouth. Those kids at this school are a bad influence.

She was sposed to pick me up.

Get in this cab.

He got inside the cab. The driver pulled off.

How come we can't take the train? He spoke to the moving window, the moving world.

We have no reason to take the train.

I'm being frank.

Please be quiet.

He obliged. Quiet and caught, the living moment before him and behind. He tried to imagine Blunt's face and received the taste of steel on his tongue. He let his violence fly free like the soaring El cars above, a flock of steel birds rising out of a dark tunnel, into bright air, the city shrinking below.

The cab slowed and felled his desires. Slim currents of traffic congealed into a thick pool up ahead. The taxi advanced an inch or two every few minutes. The El's skeletal structure rose several stories above them. An occasional train rumbled by and shook the cab and mocked his frail yearning. He looked out the window to vent his anger. A good ways off he could discern a woman standing in a building doorway, a guitar strapped to her body and a coffee can at her gym-shoed feet. Coatless, in a checkered cotton dress, her bare muscular legs as firm as the El's pylons in the bitter cold. She kept rhythm with one foot, while some lensed smiling face rose or fell with each stroke of the guitar.

He shouldered the cab door open and started through the street, his boots breaking through snow at each step, and traffic so thick he had to squeeze between the cars. Wind tried to push him back, and the fat snowsuit wedged between two parked cars. But he freed himself from the moment and thought of his mother and thought of his father and thought of the preacher and thought of Blunt and fancy clothes and contact lenses and lahzonyah and smiles and promises.

Hatch! Mamma shouted after him, her voice distant, weak, deformed, small, dwarfish, alien. Intent on his target, he moved like a tank in his armored snowsuit, smooth heavy unstoppable anger.

Close now. Blunt framed in the doorway, his face trained on her guitar. Her hair was not long and flowing and silver but knotted in a colorless bun. Her eyes were not green or blue or brown or gray but a dull black. She shut them. Aimed her pug nose, arrowlike, at the El platform. Snapped open her mouth.

> *Baby, baby, take off this heavy load*
> *Oh, baby, baby, lift up my heavy load*
> *Got this beast of burden*
> *And he got to go.*

Quick legs, he stepped up onto the curb and almost tilted over in the heavy snowsuit. He kicked the coffee can like a football, coins rising and falling like metal snow, then crouched low and charged like a bull. He felt wood give under his head and loose splinters claw his face. He fought to keep his balance, loose coins under his feet, and in the same instant found himself flailing his hands and arms against Blunt's rubber-hard hips and legs. Gravity wrestled him down. Dazed, he shook his head clear, gathered himself in a scattering moment, and looked up at Blunt. Her lined face. Her pug nose. Her stork mouth. And the strapped guitar that hung from her body—broken wood, twisted wire, useless metal—like some ship that had crashed into a lurking giant.

His eyes met hers, black, stunned. Wait, she said. You don't understand. She shook her head. You don't—

I hate you! he screamed. I hate you! Concrete shoved him to his feet. I hate you! Brutal wind pulled him into motion and led him as if he were leashed. Down the sidewalk, beyond the El's steel pylons, through warped, unfamiliar streets.

Dog Tags

Begin with . . . rock.
End with water.
– THEODORE ROETHKE

Through a window fogged with his breath, Hatch can see the first
and last cars at once as the train curls slowly around the mountain,
a giant horseshoe, the other cars—he counts them—like a string
of scattered islands, an archipelago. In the green valley below, grass
ducks under bladed wind, and trees are naked for all to see, their
skinny arms pointing in jumbled directions. The mountain curves
up from the valley in a range of stony ridges like knuckles and joints,
a peach fuzz of morning light growing from them. Up ahead, the
engine disappears into a tunnel, followed by one car, then another.
A steady rush of squeezing darkness.

Boy, take this here jar of applesauce to Mr. John Brown. Blunt held
out a mason jar, in conventional use a container for storing fruit but
in Hatch's hands a glass zoo for displaying fireflies, holes punched
in the lid, metal gills.

Yes'm. His grandmother often entrusted him with such errands.

Free of her, he unscrewed the lid and dipped his finger in for a
taste. Moist sauce made from apples fresh from Blunt's yard. He

walked past John Brown's old red pickup truck, parked on the gravel road, as still as his gray metal mailbox with its little red metal flag. He unlatched the chain-link gate and entered the tree-shadowed yard. He sensed tingling animal smell.

John Brown's house was exactly like Blunt's—except that hers was green and white, his blue and white—a long and wide cereal box knocked flat. Hatch banged on the door with practical knowledge. John Brown was hard of hearing. Almost immediately, the door wedged open, inner light spilling out, as if John Brown had been awaiting him in his heavy black shoes, dark brown slacks with sharp creases like raised tents, and crisp white shirt ringed with sweat under the armpits. John Brown poked out his head. A long narrow wasplike face. Hair cropped close, watermelon meat chewed down to the rind. Oil glistening on the scalp. Walnut-colored skin that brightened like a lightning bug in the sun. Hardly a trace of eyebrow, just two dirty smudges. Toothless mouth, puckered, drawstring tight. Razor-slit eyes. Expectant shine.

Blunt send you some applesauce. He screamed the words. She need to send two or three more jars. John Brown was starvation skinny, on the verge of disappearing.

He took the mason jar. Boy, tell Miss Pulliam I thank her kindly.

Yes, suh— But John Brown had already slammed the door shut, bringing a showering of dust down from the porch roof.

Miss Bee pulled a lump of snuff from her mouth and patted it on his cheek. He closed his eyes at the pain.

Hold it in place.

It hurt.

Hold it in place.

He did as instructed, felt his cheek rising under his fingers, swollen like an overstuffed nest.

Keep it on there two hours.

Yes'm.

Two hours.

Yes'm.

If it's not better in the morning, I guess we'll have to amputate.

His mouth went tight with concentration.

And keep away from them hedges.

Bent forward in his padded adult-sized seat, he feels light move like hands up and down his back, his face hot with friction against the window's baked vibrating glass. For as far as he can see, sun covers the world, as thick as honey, a warm buttery yellow over candy-colored houses. Midgets slosh through the valley in rhythmic black duck boots. He is certain that they are singing. A hunting song. They aim their rifles at the sky—a bright shimmering pink—hammers cocked.

Light splinters against the glass and brings a sense of space into the cramped coach. He studies a line of mountains—he has seen many mountains today—and, beyond the mountains, pure distance, until a stiff breeze pushes against the window and breaks his concentration. It continues, a violent rhythm pounding for entry.

Topped with off-white shades and hanging fringes, antique lamps cast soft triangular glow, fine radiance suspended like spiderwebs in the corners. Miss Bee's store was so dim you had to carry light in from outside, massage it into your eyes. The store proper was pushed back to the farthest room of the house, money hidden in a drawer. A cigar box and a pad and pencil served as Miss Bee's cash register. An old display case as her counter. Rolls of belly fat pushed her inches from its edge. This woman, akin to no other. Hamster-fat cheeks stuffed with snuff under the constant violence of big greedy horse teeth. She watched you with big round-lidded frog eyes, her face framed by two long skinny snakelike braids. The smell inside the house-store the same as that outside: chicken shit and the stinking ghosts of unborn chicks. Miss Bee had a rooster to crow for day, and plenty of noisy chickens running about her yard, pecking secret codes into the dirt. Every now and then, some lone fowl would escape and wander out onto the gravel road, and you would chase it down.

Thank you, boy. Now, pick you out a sucka.

Thank you, ma'am. That one there.

You a good boy, ain't you?

Yes'm.

Miss Bee released a space-filling laugh.

She would come to your grandmother's house smelling like chicken and bearing gifts of food: turdlike yams, runny mashed potatoes, gummy pound cake, warmed-over greens, or a green egg—tree growing inside—from the green womb of one of her hens.

You would crack the eggs and pour the yolks into a big bowl of milk. Blunt would fork bread into the mixture, then fry the slices in a popping skillet. You ate six slices of green French toast and six strips of bacon in a puddle of thick syrup. Chewed slowly, seeking out words in the yeast and meat.

A rattle of rain, hard, slamming, glancing with wind, big crystal-like drops shattering against the window. Then bright light spoking through the clouds. A rainbow formed, a pot of gold at either end to weigh it down, keep it earthbound. Leprechauns leaped at the colored bands with open hands.

Seated inside the deep tub, he extended his arms winglike, grabbed the hard enamel sides, and tried to pilot the vessel forward. The claw-feet dug porcelain talons into the bathroom tiles.

Boy, soap yo rag real good. Blunt stood near the sink, a big washcloth folded over her palm and hanging down to her forearm like loose pizza dough.

Yes'm.

And soap that rag good over yo whole body.

Yes'm.

And be sure to wash yo elephant snout.

He set three quarters ringing on the counter. Miss Bee's eyes wandered round in her head. Should he slap them still? He wanted to.

Blunt want some bread.

Miss Bee fetched the bread.

He slapped a nickel on the counter. And give me one of them suckas. Strawberry.

Miss Bee looked him full in the face. Boy, where yo manners?

Ma'am?

Give me.

Sorry, ma'am. May I have a sucka? Please.

Miss Bee dug inside her nose, pulled her finger free, and with the same booger finger shoveled a plastic-wrapped sucker out of the box.

Broccoli-like clumps of squat tightly leaved trees and lanky palms—or so he figures; flora not native to this part of the country, the world—prodigious fronds spilling down like dreadlocks, floppy dog ears. Then black ink-lined trees traced on a thin gray-and-pink-cloud sky. Other trees in the valley, heavy with birds—he discovers three or four rare finds, new species, never before recorded by man—photo-still cows, and white houses hemmed in by blue sky, shining, naked bulbs. He fidgets in his seat, hard to keep still. A big sleek silver bird with streamlined feathers and sparkling talons lifts off into sky against the wind's resistant slap, light forming a bright badge of achievement on its breast. Earth cannot restrain it. It flies off to somewhere behind the sun.

A farmer leads a lone cow off into a clump of bushes while the other cows stand and look on. Hatch sings,

My dog resembles a badger
My dog resembles a fox
My dog resembles a bear
But my dog most resembles a dog.

He turns his eyes away from the sight. Sealed in, coach sounds.

And get out that road. Blunt snapped her umbrella open to ward off the sun. He moved under its shade and watched Blunt, her false teeth as bright as cell bars, dead person's hair concealing gray wire springs poking from her bald scalp. Not in use, the fake hair covered a white faceless squeaking Styrofoam head, like a bird perched in a tree, waiting to lift up its hairy wings and flap away. Mouth free, the teeth slept at the bottom of a mason jar like some strange fish.

Just up the road, John Brown sat on his porch, a look of worry creasing his face. It was a rare sight to see him unguarded in the open. His house was a fort, with squat flowerpots under every window—booby-trapped sentinels—and padded curtains. Even the sun was not welcome. A rare sight indeed. You might spy him in his yard, mowing down millions of green aliens with his ancient cutting machine. Blunt greeted him gladly in the hot afternoon. How you dooch?

Fine.

All right. Boy, where yo manners?

How you, John Brown? Hatch leaned out from the umbrella into the sun.

Fine, boy. Jus fine.

Hatch pepped up his step, the sun circling overhead, heat rising from the ground through his sneakers. Trucks and cars went speeding past—the drivers finding time to wave—rippling the heavy blanket of heat, but the air that circulated was no cooler. Blunt hard-breathed behind him.

Boy, slow down. You catch heatstroke.

Yes'm.

And get back in this shade.

Feet raised and her head arched back—chair and body, a curve of wave—Mamma sleeps beside him, lips quivering with the drive of her snoring, breath regulating itself, deep and slow, lines bunched on her forehead. Windows throw even shadows on her face, moving, a tiny black train. Her mouth makes a swampy sound. He builds a nest around her. Piles high all the reasons she should stay.

I wanna shake.

Miss Bee make you a shake.

Nawl. I wanna go to Chinaman's.

Go on to Miss Bee.

I don't want no Miss Bee shake.

Boy, why you so hardheaded?

Hatch watched his feet. He could kick her.

Spoiled. Just spoiled. She done spoiled you.

His line of sight traveled the floor to her sandaled toes, the corns like tiny missiles.

Here. Blunt put the dollar in his palm. You get yo float, but you go to Miss Bee and buy some dranks.

I don't want no pop. Want some tea.

Don't be so hard-headed.

Suitcases in hand, they moved slowly through the station, their heels clicking on the tiled floor. He stepped over a puddle of saliva.

How come Blunt baptize her teeth?

What?

How come she wear dead hair? He watched the tight purse of Mamma's lips.

Sometimes you think of the silliest things.

They moved through the station, the air heavy and white, coating the tongue and lips like milk, light sifting through the cloth-shaded windows like flour. Mamma's head bobbed up and down from fatigue.

You need a break, he said. You need rest.

She did not answer.

Blunt smiled as they stepped out the station—an ancient woman, by Hatch's most recent calculations, a bundle of dried sticks brittle to the touch.

The next morning, Mamma woke with a nosebleed from the heat.

Will you stay? he asked.

You know I can't.

Why not?

I have to—

You never stay.

She watched him, her chin tucked into her chest, like a boxer.

Hatch quit the house and ran over the dew-filled grass, diamond wetness that vanished in the fingers when touched. Bush and weed reached greedily after him. Gnats bunched into black fists. He mounted his bike, Blunt screaming after him, her words bouncing off his blind back: Boy, slow down. You catch heatstroke. And there was John Brown, standing in his yard, face pointed up at a green canopy of tree. Drawn by the bike's motion, he aimed his face at Hatch, his chin hard and straight, his eyes sparkling for a moment as if struggling for recognition. Come here, boy. Hatch felt a stirring in the air, a sense of his own weightlessness, a low rising on winged feet. He pumped his legs with all he had and made off. Time flew fast, for he traveled as far as his two legs and two wheels could carry him, to the outskirts of the green and brown world, where he saw, felt, and studied objects and events he believed no other had. (He would speak his finds on one condition: convincing pay.) He returned to his outpost in the dead hours of heat, tired, hunger chewing up his belly, and saw Miss Bee's familiar slow steps on the road, gravel crunching underfoot. She would be slower still after a full evening of conversation with Blunt. Hey there, boy. Fingers probing his hair, cold snakes. Together, they walked the two splintery planks—swoll up from the heat like two punch-inflicted eyes but bridge sturdy, bridge steady—leading to Blunt's front yard, Hatch guiding Miss Bee by the angle of her elbow with one hand, his other balancing his forsaken bike alongside him, and Miss Bee singing,

Got on the train
Didn't have no fare
But I rode some
I rode some

Conductor asked me
What I'm doing there
But I rode some
I rode some.

How yall? The words floated down on them from John Brown's porch.

Fine, Miss Bee said.

Sho is hot.

Ain't it the truth.

Hatch led Miss Bee through Blunt's screened front door. She was slow, and a sampling of bugs entered with her.

How you dooch?

Blunt and Miss Bee hugged.

The two women spent hours on the couch, shifting their weight from time to time—their thighs sticking to the plastic covers—and spinning talk from the loom of their wrinkled faces, thin laughter trailing across the room to the deep chair where Hatch sat, waiting, reeling in the clear flow of words, sneakers two feet above the floor, jerking, wiggling, and throbbing like hooked fish. The women used tall glasses of clinking iced tea to quench their fiery tongues, cool them to momentary rest. Then they started again. Miss Bee's armpits raised a staying odor, a thick hot pressure that filled Hatch's chest.

Why she smell like that?

She can't help it.

She got plenty of deodorant right there in her store.

She can't help it. She sick.

On the sly, he pinched his nose. Thinking, why don't she pack up her tongue and go home?

Boy, help me to the gate, she would say, rubbing her peach seed–hard fingers on his head, her heavy bowling-pin legs made light by two wings of sweat spread across the back of her dark blue housedress.

You see all them sacks in the backa his truck?

Yes, Lawd.

Hatch too recalled seeing a high stack of grocery bags in the back of John Brown's red pickup, wheels flat with the weight.

Yes, Lawd.

Must have a tapeworm in his belly.

And still ain't got no meat on his bones.

And don't he know better than to leave food out like that.

Maybe he like it that way. Rotten.

Wouldn surprise me one bit. Not one.

Hatch sank deeper into the chair.

He got fever in his feathers, for sho.

Hatch pictured a chicken, feathers aflame.

He shell-shocked.

Hatch pictured a shelled green bean and a green shock of corn.

He touched, fo sho.

Hatch pictured a bullying finger plucking a forehead.

They shoulda put him away a long time ago.

Um-huh. If you got a broken leg, walk it off. But you can't walk off yo head.

But for the grace of God.

Yes. Grace. Miss Bee made signs in the air above her head.

John Brown peeked through the triple-chained crack in the door.

Hatch inched backward. Blunt wanna know if you carry her to town?

Boy, tell Miss Pulliam I carry her. John Brown shut the door.

Hatch ran so fast that he almost fell, his feet twisting against the porch steps. He liked John Brown's truck, riding up front in the high cab. So he served Blunt the reply, then darted back to the road and waited for John Brown in the truck's thick shadow. No sooner had he positioned himself against the sun-heated metal than did John Brown appear in his doorway, appear on his ancient porch, rotating the brim of his hat in the circle of his fingers. He set his shoulders broad and moved slow over the cement walk to the gravel road, shirt buttons glowing like bulbs.

Blunt reached the road with her most youthful gait. John Brown quickened his pace—his shoes light—stepping on the very toes, walking on long black knives. He opened the passenger-side door for Blunt and Hatch—Thank you, John Brown—and shut it, with the clang of a lock, after they got in; then he got in himself, the three of them now in the front seat—the only seat—of the truck, Hatch sandwiched between John Brown and Blunt, rigid, perfectly straight. John Brown gave off a fresh rain scent that had soaked deep into his skin. The cab smelled of electrical wires, flaking leather, old rubber, and rust. Hatch's skin felt tight, the whole world squeezing in. For the first time he hungered for the truck's square open space, out back. John Brown worked his fingers near the dashboard, and the engine sputtered, the groan of ignition, air from a balloon. Gears screeched for traction, then they set off over the gravel, John Brown's big black shoe on the accelerator and brake, his long narrow eyes (like string beans—nigger Chinese, Blunt called them) fixed on the road, as steady as headlights, unblinking. He kept the truck at a crawl, both hands on the huge steering wheel, big thunderous tires roaring through the glassy heat of the streets, the truck shivering like a wet dog. The anchor of John Brown's heavy-shoed foot kept it squarely on the road.

Ain't seen brogans like that since Moses, Miss Bee said.

Two tugboats, Blunt said.

Two tanks.

Frogs.

Dawgs.

Hawgs.

Dust sifted off the rusted metal in a fine light brown cloud.

Sure is hot, Miss Pulliam.

Yes, suh, Blunt said. You got that right.

Must be firing up the ovens in hell, Hatch signifying to himself.

Like to catch heatstroke. Blunt smiled.

Steam-cleaning the pitchforks.

Hot day like this, no way that monkey come down from that tree.

Blunt's elastic smile snapped and broke.

Miss Pulliam, you know anything bout getting a monkey outta a tree?

Why, no, suh.

Well, I might chunk a rock.

Try one of yo big-ass shoes.

Now, there's a thought.

Can that monkey drive? Hatch said, subdued.

Blunt's head spun on her neck like an oiled machine. She gave him an unflinching, icy look.

Boy, John Brown said, you old enough to know that no monkey don't know nothing bout no driving.

Maybe he got his own car. A monkeymobile.

Boy—

How long you had this truck? Hatch asked.

This truck old as me, and I ain't no spring chicken. Mo like a lazy winter dog.

How old is that?

Blunt's eyes swelled at him, red, heavy, ripe apples.

These kids fulla questions. If God wanted young folks to be smart, he woulda made em grown.

They passed a junkyard, overturned cars like playful dogs, paws up.

Now, I got a question for you.

Suh?

You know what a horse is?

Hatch said nothing for a moment. You mean that animal?

Yes. Now, what a horse is?

Suh?

That's a pig that don't fly straight.

John Brown's laughter crashed against the windshield, then thinned out to a few snorts and grunts.

Cold light barely warms him through the moving glass. He sneezes. Fog beginning to curl around the valley. Night coming on hard, the sun dropping low and red through the mountains. The sky grows pink then purple. Trees arrowed off into dark heaven.

And there is more to see. Stars, sparkling teeth. The moon, a fierce white pendulum. Red buzzing traffic and squat houses with fat black iron bars on the doors and windows. City lights on the horizon, earthbound stars. The coach glowing, shadows springing to life.

He applies the wool blanket to his body like a fuzzy second skin.

Then the moon swings at him, a bright slice of it cutting cleanly through the window. He feels his head for wetness, for blood.

Boy, come here.

Suh?

Come here.

Hatch did not move.

You gon run off? Well, gon, if you want.

Blood went thick behind his eyes. John Brown awaited him in the tree's shade. His lined wrinkled body seemed to be cracking, fragmenting, into puzzle pieces of shadow. Hatch was not afraid. He needed to see, he wanted to see. He got down from his bike, slow and deliberate. His feet moved even more slowly over the gravel, as silent as house slippers. He opened the metal latch of John Brown's gate, entered the yard, and let the latch close behind him with a clanging sound like that of a crowbar against a radiator.

See the monkey?

The day calm and vacant. Full afternoon heat. A few fluffy white buffalo clouds. John Brown's face and chin jutted up at the tree, his eyes closed. He put movement in his body. Slow, a riverboat— plodding along blindly to some hidden rhythm, bent forward against the still and heavy heat, face blank and empty.

Hatch inched backward.

John Brown stepped from the tree's shade into bright light, rag-gedly breathing, as if he had just completed a cross-continental swim. He opened his eyes—sun in the pupils, two horizons—and thrust his face close. To see Hatch better? Photograph his thoughts?

Boy, I ask you a question.

Flying spit peppered Hatch's cheeks. Words hovered, rising, steamlike, from John Brown's bright face. An ancient face criss-crossed with stiff wrinkles, rusty rails. The old man's long rigid fin-ger pointed up into thick foliage, where a wide blade of light slashed through the leaves. Hatch looked in wonder. Squinted into the flaming green.

The sky relaxed. Then he saw it, the monkey. Tiny eyes looking off into the clouds. Shoulders hunched up to its ears. Tail hooked over a branch. A hanging ornament.

The monkey shuddered, stirred.

My God! John Brown said. All gravity lifted from his face. His mouth fell open, unhinged.

The monkey took a deep breath, then extended his wings in the sun, which lit them like screens, put them on display. Hatch could see every tracing of vein—miniature roads—every bumpy muscle, and the delicate framework of bone under the skin. The wings were thin, almost transparent.

With effortless arrogance, the monkey began moving his wings backward and forward—all comfort and ease, the wings light and flexible—a timed and measured fanning that gradually built up to a quick and constant haze that caused the air around Hatch to quiver, his heart to beat without mercy.

Toilet Training

I

Few cars and fewer people. The sun perched, hawklike, on a rooftop corner. The sky blue and silent. Hatch gazed into the rich expanse of his shadow and felt challenged. Something flared up inside him. With spring in his legs, he bolted through the strange but familiar constellation of streets. A strong staying breeze, an uneven blowing at his ears. His eyes straining against their sockets, needles pricking his lungs, and the sidewalk grabbing for his ankles. He ducked inside a doorway and sat down hard on the stoop. Head bowed, feverish, he struggled within.

The sun grinned down. What up, homes?

Hatch removed the water pistol from inside his jacket pocket, shielded his eyes, and sighted along the barrel. Curled his finger around the trigger and gently squeezed. The sun steamed from the blast of cool liquid, trembled, but remained lodged on the rooftop. Frowned down into Hatch's face and spewed sharp angles of light in retaliation. Hatch drew back, defeated.

A small figure moved in the hollow of an autumn afternoon. Jacket, a backward apron; sleeves tied around his waist. The sun waited, half-swallowed by the horizon. But he walked quietly, drawing reassurance into himself with each step, his sneaky shadow slithering along behind him.

II

Cosmo squats behind the hedge, claws dangling at his groin like wicked catcher's mitts. The dome of his head visible above the green edge, a half-risen half-fallen sun. His hair crinkled and greasy like fried bacon. The sky brightens. Sunlight darts inside the hedge. Dungarees ignite, boots glisten. A rat scuttles through the grass, unaware.

In one movement, Cosmo crashes through the hedge, lands, froglike, and levels a claw. The rat is still and lumpy, a sack of loose rocks. Cosmo rubs his claws with joy. The rodent recovers and rushes for the grass. Too late.

Cosmo snatches up his prey, cranes his neck, and begins lowering the rat headfirst into his mouth. The rat's front feet pedal in air. Buckteeth snap at Cosmo's lips. But the front feet and the buckteeth and the head disappear inside Cosmo's mouth, a fuzzy sword. A gurgling sound announces its descent. The butt wiggles. The hind feet stroke Cosmo's cheeks. The tail whips.

Cosmo blinks, hard, squaring his mouth. The feet twitch a little. Cosmo brings both claws to his mouth and forces the rat inside, its tail gyrating between his lips. He sucks it up like a string of spaghetti, throat pregnant.

Carpet, coffee table, chairs, love seats, paintings, couch, and walls— all submerged in the liquid glow of television, which thins out, a few blue- white strands, ghostly ripples, the farther it travels from the source.

How come those Indians don't pull out they arrows? Hatch asks. Is they chicken?

Nawl, Cosmo says. If they pull out they arrows, then those cowboys will come back to life.

If Cosmo regurgitates the rat, will it come back to life?

He scratches away spittle with a bladed fingernail, long, sharp, and shiny in the sunlight. Continues to squat, awaiting birth.

III

A thick fuzzy night. Coming out of the hot street, made hotter by a golden low-hanging moon and hundreds of blazing streetlamps. Hatch pushed the door open with his fingertips, the water pistol tight in his other hand. He entered and closed the door behind him. Wide-eyed in the darkness. Mamma was usually home to greet him when he made it in from school. On rare occasions Cosmo would arrive before her. At the far end of the room, French doors, open just enough for one to edge through sideways. A sliver of slanted light, a thin line of carpet luminous. The jacket still tight about his waist, Hatch pushed his keys deep inside his pocket, then wrapped both hands around the water pistol and walked toward the beacon of light. The dark put a hand against his back and shoved. He fell heavy to the floor, hammer to anvil, chin-first, pistol still in hand, the weapon plowing a short path through the carpet, raking up fibers. He shut his eyes against the pain. Spun his head and laid his jowl against the plush springy softness of the carpet. Shook inside as if some strange force were gathering.

Sometimes you just irritate the shit out of me. Cosmo started round.

Hatch raised his head and flicked open his eyes. Something stepped into the edge of his vision in the angle of light. He didn't move. Followed the something with his eyes. Blinked in details. Old-man shoes. Sharply pointed. With whorls of perforation. Baggy pants with fine creases. Knee-length blazer. Silk polka-dot tie. Fedora. Hatch's body trembled with something it could not let out.

Yo! In front of him now, glaring down.

The pistol was ice between his palms.

Yo!

I'm all right!

I didn't ask if you was all right.

So.

Say what?

He didn't say anything.

Did you say something?

Nawl.

Cosmo flexed his soles, stretching the leather, talons threatening to burst out. I didn't think so. He threw the door wide. Shadows fled. Hatch waited until he was absolutely certain that Cosmo had quit the room, then squeezed his eyes tight.

IV

That's why I say, Mamma said, her voice a whisper, only what you have in your stomach is yours. She placed her spoon on the edge of her saucer and raised her cup to her lips, her face a smooth round tab of caramel candy.

What can you do? Dad said, head as bald as the chicken drumstick in his fist, torso constricted in a tight sports shirt, arms strong, with pronounced veins. What can you do?

They were seated next to one another at the long dining table, framed within the long window behind them, night pressing against the light within, the faraway rush and hum of occasional cars. On the opposite side, Cosmo sat beside Hatch, stretching out first one leg and then the other and feeling inside each trouser pocket. The smell of meat bent in the air, and Cosmo's cologne snapped in and out of Hatch's nostrils like a sporadic cloud of gnats.

Mamma glared at Hatch over the edge of her cup. He placed the water pistol on his lap, sat back. Cosmo was fussing with his tie, straightening it, smoothing out the wrinkles. Mamma threw her eyes in his direction. What's wrong? A hundred-dollar bill slip in there?

Cosmo grinned. No, ma'am.

Well then.

Cosmo picked up his fork and started in on his dinner.

Hatch mumbled grace—God good. God great. Let us thank him for food and men—and lifted his fork. The plates and cups and utensils were white from constant scrubbing. He studied his distorted reflection.

Poor man. To spend all those years in jail. And for nothing. Mamma sipped steaming liquid. Hatch admired the rhythm of her throat. Dad opened his mouth to admit corn bread. Cosmo did not look up from his plate. A splash of light from the small chandelier above the dinner table gave his hair an even greasier appearance. Mamma lowered her cup to the saucer. An innocent man. But God will tell.

Cosmo fumbled his fork.

God will tell.

Cosmo raised his head and stared fixedly, straight past Dad's shoulder and through the window.

Mamma took a cigarette—smoking was her only vice—from her pack on the table. Lit up, drew long and deep, blew out a stream of smoke. Such was her sustenance, for she put their hunger before her own, waited for *her men* to eat before she forked her fill. She wanted her men healthy and strong, and daily prepared each a tall cold glass of sulfur and water, filmed over with cod-liver oil, and watched and waited until each drained it in her monitoring presence. Now he's back with his family.

Cosmo stared straight ahead—out the window? at a precise location in the black distance?

Mamma drew on the cigarette, blew the smoke through her nose like a bull. Hatch considered applauding the miracle but decided against it. She set the cigarette on the lip of her saucer. And they gave him money. Millions of dollars. But what he had to endure! His eye poked out! Wit a red-hot poker!

Cosmo sat, transfixed.

Mamma took a sip of coffee—what Hatch had been waiting for, that rhythm; he had to clamp his hand over his mouth to keep from screaming in delight—and lowered her cup to the saucer. But see, God will tell. They been tryin to put that company back to right. But they never will. Never will. Mamma shook her head in righteous satisfaction.

Now, that's my idea of justice, Cosmo said.

Mamma's mouth snapped shut. In one fluid motion, she surged forward and landed a sonorous blow against Cosmo's jaw.

Hatch felt a curious stillness in the room, some invisible tent attached to the ceiling and overhanging the table. A bean dropped from Dad's raised stationary fork.

Thank you, Cosmo said. He scooted his chair back, rose quickly, and quit the table, creases snapping.

Something rolled coldly down Hatch's cheek. He struggled to see. Mamma cut her eyes toward him. You want some? she said, still perched over the table.

No, ma'am. He wiped his eyes, darted a glance, swung his legs back and forth.

Mamma sat down. In counterpoint, Dad sprang up so quickly that he almost fell to the floor—as if the chair had been snatched out from under him. His sharp footsteps clipped down the hall. Mamma lit another cigarette and puffed slowly and deeply in another world, behind thin bars of smoke.

Shades drawn to prevent the moon from surveying him through the window. Cosmo lay flat on his bed, staring up at the ceiling, studying the heavens through the telescope of his dick.

V

Yo brother retarded.

Don't talk bout my family.

Yo brother—
My final warning.
And he—
Hatch punches the bastard in the mouth.

A crew of roughnecks on the corner spots Cosmo, his fedora bobbing on his head like a storm-tossed ship. What up, player. They laugh, throwing their heads back.

Go ask yo mamma! Hatch shouts. Stank ho.
Cosmo looks at him hard. Jus mind yo own business.
You gon let them talk bout you?
Cosmo slaps him upside the head.
See the way that gump slap shorty?
Yeah. Picking on the lil guy.
We should kick his ass.
Give him a fo-real ass whupping.
Hatch rubs his pain-blotted head.
Come on, Cosmo says.
Skinny motherfucker.
Stick in the mud.
Retard.
Gump.

VI

Hatch sucker punches Dad in his hard flat middle and pleads for a cupla bucks. Dad watches Hatch with large quizzical eyes. What? he says. A cupla bucks? Here. Dad hops once, twice, kicking his heels into the middle of his back. Grins. He tells Hatch to rub his bald peanut-colored head for good luck. Lets Hatch tug his beard. Then he digs deep inside his pockets—he sounds them with silver—and gives Hatch *three* dollars. Stiff new bills, brightly inked. Vibrant, Dad's dress shirt glows like a movie screen. (Mamma keeps his ironed tops in the refrigerator so they'll remain soft and wrinkle free.) He heads for the door, his trusty Leica hanging from a neck strap.

Sargent, Mamma says, leave that camera here. Some thug mistake you for a tourist.

I can't. You know it's the eye of fortune.

Well, at least put it in the case.

Dad complies, then folds his red silk handkerchief into a compact square and polishes the brass door knocker. Joyous in alligator shoes, stepping carefully down the street on tippytoes—the inflated balls of his feet—taking small steps as if avoiding shit-smeared concrete.

The sun kisses the street into light and color. Skyscrapers glazed in bronze, copper, and gold. Hard haze on the brick buildings, cooking all the folks inside. Ants fry in the dirt. Roaches explode like tiny grenades. Nothing settles or stays untouched.

Dad cannot bear a single finger of warmth. Year-round keeps on his person a portable battery-operated fan that buzzes like a miniature bomb. An air conditioner cools every room in the house, humming at all hours, around the clock, a high cold winter voice.

One telling day, heat rips out the power lines. Agitation at heart, Dad seals himself inside his Town Car, parked at the curb in front of the house. Hatch watches him from a high window in the two-car garage where Cosmo lives and studies and works.

Ain't you gon come?

Nawl. Cosmo tinkers with an engine. You go head.

What's wrong? Is you chicken?

Nawl, I ain't chicken.

Then let's go.

I'm fine right here. Got work to do. Plenty work.

Chicken.

Cosmo's hands move over the engine.

Chicken.

Punk, who you calling chicken?

You. Chicken.

Cosmo looks at Hatch, fire in his eyes.

Hatch lowers his face. Backs off. Best not to push his luck. He runs, legs pumping, to the Town Car and finds Mamma standing on the driver's side, leaning over, face level with the window, her long heavy breasts hanging like rubber bands, a prim dress billowing about her sculpted calves, her high long heels sharp tools jackhammering the concrete floor, her rich behind raised for all the world to see. Hatch bites his tongue in knowledge. Eye to keyhole, he sees Dad bang her at night—Kiss me, my proud beauty—Dad's duty, bed swinging from side to side like a hammock.

Sargent.

When will the power be on? Dad says, neck stiff, veins bulging like electrical cables. He stares straight ahead through the windshield. The car's roof glazed in afternoon sun. The air conditioner wheezing against the glass.

I just called the electric company, Mamma says. It'll be at least a few hours.

Well, I'll just stay in here until they get it back on.

Sargent, don't act a fool. I—

I'll stay out here. Rolling his eyes a little to raise the volume of his voice.

Bright sun forces Hatch to blink. Up and down the street, trees shake in a hot breeze, light dripping, sweatlike, from their leaves.

Then I'll sit out here with you.

No. Sun on Dad's face, a small glowing window.

Sargent, let me keep you company.

No.

Don't act a fool.

Dad doesn't speak or move, eyes staring straight ahead. A feeling silence.

Well, can I get you anything? A nice cold glass of aloe vera juice?

The sun hits Dad's bald head with a dull thud. His shaped goatee glows like vanilla ice cream. No.

Why don't you drive around some, Hatch says.

Mamma looks at him. Go in the house. Hatch doesn't move. Boy, don't make me use my belt. Hatch starts his legs. Mamma turns back to Dad, whose blank face gleams. Sargent.

He says nothing. Deaf. Oblivious.

Open the door.

Narrows his eyes and clenches his fists on the stationary steering wheel.

VII

Cosmo leans around the corner, cautious. He looks back and takes Hatch's hand. Come on. They move swiftly to the bathroom. Cosmo leans outside the door, takes another look around, face bunched as if a firecracker had just exploded near his ears. He straightens up, tears off a square of toilet paper, crumples it into a ball, and pushes it into Hatch's hand. Here. He gets himself some. He carefully places the balled-up toilet paper into his mouth, then chews like an old man. Go on. Hatch pops the white ball into his mouth. Cosmo tears another sheet from the roll.

Mamma touches Cosmo's hair, slick wonder. Grease glistens on her fingertips. She rubs them together like money. You think you Mr. Cool in that bebop suit. She looks Cosmo up and down. He keeps his head bowed, thumb and forefinger shaping the brim of his fedora. Look like a pimp.

I ain't no pimp.

What you say?

Nothing.

Wait till your father hear bout this.

Cosmo stands there, head bowed.

You know I'm gon tell him.

If you must.

Mamma scrunches up her face. Let me advise you. Detest who you are. Build a better self.

VIII

Six o'clock. The alarm trumpets. Hatch lies very still in his bed until he hears Cosmo's door shut. He throws back his quilts, leaps up, opens his own door, and tiptoes down the hall. Bends over slow and careful to avoid knocking his forehead against the doorknob. Peers, squint-eyed, through the circle of the keyhole. Cosmo throws his clothes into a bundle, onto the floor, picks up a book, and slides into bed, genitals swinging. Hatch had hoped for something more.

After a while, Cosmo puts the book aside, then slips beneath the covers. Squirms on his belly, reptilelike, to get comfortable. Imprisoned in shoe boxes under the bed, rats squeak like heels on a basketball court.

His room is sorely neglected. The garage is his domain, where he spends most of the night on a queen-sized mattress on a patch of floor clean of oil stains and gasoline. Space arranged in an order he works hard to maintain. Something about the colors and their careful placement suggests motion. Dozens of stacks of aviation books and technical magazines. Engines in various stages of repair. Mechanical refuse from the neighbors' trash and yards. On the regular he invites Hatch into his world, his secrets. Kodaks of a woman with two assholes. A six-tittied dwarf. A man with a big fat titty where his dick should be. And other wonders: A glow-in-the-dark penis. A crystal vagina. Aluminum condoms. Specimens in fluid-filled mason jars. He offers these revelations with a straight face, hot sunshine pouring through the high single window. Hatch aims through the glass and shoots down flying saucers with his water gun.

Want to hear something? Cosmo asks.

What?

This one time, I ate a whole bar of scented soap. For the heck of it.

What happened?

For a whole week, my turds come out white and smellin like expensive perfume.

Seven o'clock. Hatch rushes to his door, parts it a little. Cosmo approaches from down the hall, underclothing tucked against his side, suit trailing behind his shoulder, old-man shoes untied, genitals swinging.

Fully dressed an hour later. Breakfast on the table. He eats in one minute flat.

Gon choke to death one day, Mamma says. Eatin like somebody crazy.

Yes'm. He kisses her cheek. Leather satchel in hand, clean dungarees folded over his arm, he rushes out to greet the new day. Walks bent forward, like somebody pushing through slanting snow.

If you gon be a pilot, how come you tinkering with that lil-bitty engine?

Cosmo cracked his knuckles, popping one at a time. Look, I ain't gon be no pilot. That's a lawn-mower engine. And, those there, Volkswagen. I'm studying power-plant mechanics. I overhaul air-cooled engines. He went on, sounding like one of his books.

Hatch kept his distance. Drew his water pistol and considered firing.

Cosmo looked him in the face, grinning at the threat, liquid danger. Opened his arms and gestured, expansively, his smile wide. These are machines for living.

Ain't you gon be a pilot?

I never said that.

What did you say?

Cosmo frowned into the bowl of his hat. I'm gon be a mechanic, a power-plant mechanic. See, they got this program at school that'll low me to get both my power-plant license and my body license.

You got five schools offering you scholarships, Mamma said.

Cosmo snapped the brim of his hat.

Dad looked steadily at him, pulling his silver-streaked goatee with long strokes of his fist.

I like to fix things.

Where you go last night?

Ma'am?

Are you deaf now too? Where did you go last night?

Nowhere.

Nowhere?

Drivin.

Drivin where?

Just drivin. Nowhere in particular.

Nowhere in particular smelling like cigarette smoke?

Cosmo keeps his eyes lowered, fedora in hand.

I don't know what path you're on, but I'll tell you this: don't swap horses in the middle of the stream.

The room shines with the shimmering of the street. Cosmo stands rigid, lean face in shadow, following with a blank look his pacing father. Though he maintains an appetite, eats his meals in greedy helpings, he has a polelike appearance, skinny arms, narrow shoulders, and no hips or buttocks. And that hungry-ass face. The only thing big on him is his hands. He looks like some mechanical figure from one of his aviation books.

I don't understand why the boy so skinny. Look like somebody over in Africa.

Dad quickens his pace. Hatch's skin grows warm with fear and excitement. Dad halts and looks Cosmo straight in the face. They are watching each other, separate nightscapes of parked vehicles and moving traffic flowing across each face.

Cosmo.

Yes, sir.

Either shit or get off the pot.

IX

You know where babies come from? Cosmo's feet make no sound on the garage floor.

Uh-huh.

Where?

Out they navel.

True. And don't let nobody tell you different.

It was a lot like sighting through a hole made by your thumb and forefinger, the metal door lock cold against your brow:

Dad lay facedown on the bed, arms around his pillow. The blankets heaved powerfully. Soft morning light painted on the shaded window. His scalp glowed with the strength of the approaching day. Mamma put her cheek on his shoulder.

I'm an angel, she said. I could dance on the head of a pin.

Hatch crawls into the bedroom and hides at the back of the closet with the door slightly ajar. A wedge of vision. Mamma rushes out of the bathroom, fully dressed. Halts before the full-length mirror, body shaking with the shock of the sudden stop. Screws her tam down well over her forehead, checks her bangs. Straightens out the things in her purse, lifts coat from the bed. Exits, buttocks seesawing.

Sargent, how come you ain't dressed for church?

I don't think I can make it today.

Sargent.

I am perfectly serious. Sincere. My joints are stiff. He demonstrates.

Sargent, please stop actin a fool. We gon be late. Don't spoil my one day of the week.

You don't understand. My joints are stiff. From the cold.

Mamma stands there with something flickering hot behind her eyes. She spins on her heels and quits the house, door slamming behind.

The batter hits a pop fly into center field. The camera tracks another player as he moves into position, glove at the ready.

I hope he misses it, Hatch says.

Why?

They always catch it. Why can't they miss sometime?

Cosmo rises from his seat next to Hatch, his audience his rundown collection of engines. In his brother, Hatch sees a prophecy of his physical-self-to-be. Mamma has dressed them like twins for church. Tall skinny Cosmo and short plump Hatch, his ventriloquist dummy.

Rest assured, Cosmo says. He flicks off the television, baseball in permanent flight. Anything you think of has happened.

What?

Anything you imagine in your brain has happened, sometime, somewhere.

Anything?

Yes.

Really?

Yes.

A woman of biblical proportions, Sistah Turner turns her back to the class and begins to chalk a lesson on the blackboard. Cosmo, in a low voice: Look at that fine ho! Hatch and fellow students double over in their seats with laughter. Sistah Turner spins. Scans the class. Cosmo casts a few mean looks to silence would-be traitors.

Sistah Turner summons the students to her desk for punishment, one by one. Sign your name on her licking stick, then assume the position. Discipline, Sistah Turner says. Say it. Hatch says it. Sistah Turner's hard paddle works on his soft butt. Later, when he arrives home, he rushes to the john, shuts and locks the door, slips down his draws, and cranes his neck, trying to see if his name is emblazoned on his behind.

Much weeping and wailing. Hatch, bottom tender, watches Cosmo angrily, contemplates betrayal. Cosmo sits with his eyes firmly shut, tightening in and out of dreams.

After class, Mamma takes her sons into a dark corner and tests for recalcitrance, extending one thin knuckle before each boy's forehead and letting it hover there, humming, seeking the necessary evidence in their eyes. She raps the guilty party with the knuckle, force and number of raps fitting the crime.

They follow Mamma into the church, her white ruffled dress billowing about her legs, waves. They glide down the red thickly carpeted aisle. Hatch steps carefully, afraid his feet will sink into the raging floor. He stumbles. Recovers his balance. A classic delinquent, Cosmo whispers to Hatch: Satan fell. The greatest disaster in the history of world aviation.

They seat themselves on a hard wooden pew, brightly polished, like a canoe. Hatch's feet dangle above the carpet's red bloody waters. Cosmo sits beside him, jaw rigid, face flattened, as if pressing into glass. Words cascade from the preacher's wine-aged lips. Hatch searches for something firm to grab on to.

Sit up straight!

That bitter and poisonous apple, that hot coal of lust in Adam's belly.

Cosmo's fingers twitch, the urgent pulse of awakening life. Cosmo whispers into Hatch's ear, I drank from a jawbone.

Hatch takes him immediately for what he seems.

The collection plate comes around for the third time—Hatch doesn't remember sitting on the pew for so long, but he has—coins like sparkling eyes, fish scales. A repetition of images, mechanical proliferation.

Out of the eater come forth meat, and out of the strong come forth sweetness.

Cosmo jerks as if to sneeze and spills his half-digested breakfast into the collection plate.

X

We discussed it. Mamma holds Cosmo in her gaze. Don't use the car no mo on Saturday nights.

What? Cheek black.

Cosmo has devised a new trick: he can hoard air inside his lungs, then blow it toward tight lips, causing one cheek to expand while the other remains flat. That paradox matched by his gait, neither a walk nor a run but a clumsy advance, leaning forward a little with his chin thrust out, straining to see something in the distance, the inflated cheek black with the heat of the straining engine inside his jaw.

Hatch watches Cosmo through the garage window. Cosmo circles about from corner to corner, crashes into the walls, bug to glowing lamp.

XI

Hatch entered through the kitchen, trying not to make any noise. He raised the water pistol and moved on. What he hoped to avoid awaited him. Cosmo was standing to one side of the chandelier, facing Hatch but staring through Hatch at some vision that Cosmo alone could see. His physical appearance confirmed what Hatch had long suspected, that a strange new life was flowering inside him. One hand jerked as if shaking dice, while the other squeezed and relaxed like tweezers opening and closing or castanets snapping.

Hatch spun and rushed back in the direction from which he had come. He bounded down the back-porch steps, almost crashed into the corner of the house as he turned, stumbled through the lawn area, cut sharply again, and leaped onto the front-porch steps. The porch light made the darkness strangely comfortable. The water pistol warm in his hand.

XII

He could feel something cold rising up in him and thought to turn back. The house taking shape as he watched from his command post in a tangle of bushes and hedges on a low hill. The darkness his shelter. Then he realized he was actually seeing an expanding architecture: the house, the garage, the street, the church, the neighborhood, the jagged-leaved trees that ate the horizon. With this small but significant finding, he felt a new confidence. In time he would face his brother.

You think you grown? What time was you sposed to be in the house?
But Cosmo been aggravatin me.
You a tattletale now?

XIII

The sun is a silver penny pasted onto the sky. A slow rain descends indifferently. Cosmo and Hatch race down the street, their speed a challenge that the sky accepts. A steady downpour. Hatch catches water on his tongue and drinks it. Cosmo hops off the curb into puddles, splashing his pointed old-man shoes, frenzied sharks.

The rain comes in gray swaths. Hatch and Cosmo cut into a doorway where others have also sought refuge. Hatch's soggy sneakers fart whenever he wiggles his toes. Cosmo turns, faces the crowd from under his fedora. Spreads his arms wide, greeting the rain. We are gathered here today . . .

Rain transforms the streets into angry rivers, swirling eddies. Hard wind slaps hats off heads. Hair flattened into a flying wave, Cosmo ducks under an awning, shoves others aside to squeeze in, create his own little bit of space, elbow room. Together they stare out silently into the street at a curtain of performing rain and a swollen gutter. Police officers wrapped in plastic direct almost stationary traffic. Cosmo shivers, building up energy for an illumination, which does not come. A full hour before the rain eases. A mocking peck of blue sky.

Morning light fell slant upon the couch, where Cosmo lay under several layers of blankets, feverish—throat clogged, eyes shut in pain—and holding his stomach like a pregnant woman.

You may be sick, but you better keep an eye on yo brother when he get home from school, Mamma said.

Sure.

Make sure he eats his dinner.

Sure.

And don't aggravate him.

Sure.

The moment the door shut, he rose from the couch, red robe and slippers flaming about him, and stood rigidly in place, the sole of one foot clamped behind his knee, and the palm of his hand masking his eyes. One cheek black and puffy, the other, colorless and tent taut. The morning opened around him and he stood erect in its center, a stamen.

A ripe day. The sky so near that Hatch drew back from its heat. The sun blinked a drunk's red eye. Red clouds stumbled. He withdrew into shadow, band upon band, bar upon bar. His hands crimson wings.

Constellations as pale as milk. Stars banged against roofs. Hatch passed the lit windows of houses, perhaps a face or two looking out from them. Then home. The porch glowed with light and softened the darkness. He moved cautiously upon the black stairs. Opened the door. Fire shot through the back of his neck.

The hard wooden floor sagged under his waterlogged spine. He squeezed back burning tears. His legs stiff. His neck stiff, caught in some unseen bear's honed teeth. How long had he been here? He turned his head and the bear bit harder. Two spotlights gawked down at him from the ceiling. A third fixture cast a cone of light on a large white sheet draped along the long window like a sail and flapping freely. The room was completely bare, all furniture gone.

Punk, get on up. I ain't got all day.

He could not see Cosmo, only hear him. He explored the back of his neck with cautious fingers, trying to pinpoint teeth, triage physical damage.

Forget yo neck.

My neck is fine!

The unseen bear teeth clamped down.

Then get up.

I ain't.

Get up.

No. You play too much.

I ain't playin. Cosmo moved somewhere in the room. He stepped into the cone of light wearing a robe and slippers, the same red robe and slippers from earlier. Eyes wide. Skin taut like burns freshly healed. And the swollen cheek, an unwanted growth. His shadow shimmered against the sheet.

Wait till Mamma see what you done. The furniture.

Cosmo stood there, eyes wide spotlights. He spread a slow grin.

I'm tellin. You gon get a whupping when Mamma get home.

Cosmo watched him for a moment. Then he tightened the cord of his robe. We got some business to take care of.

I ain't doing no business with you.

Shut up.

You can't make me.

Cosmo moved across the room with his new walk. Didn't I tell you to shut the fuck up? Bones creaking, Hatch raised himself to hands and knees. The bear matched his resistance, lodging its teeth into the bone, asserting claim. He tried to rise but found that his legs too had come under new allegiance, chained and posted traps around his ankles. He dragged himself backward into the corner, the most he could do. Cosmo reached him, slapped him upside the head.

Hatch collapsed. I'm gon tell Dad too. He covered his head with his hands.

What! Cosmo flashed a look of pure hatred. His puffy cheek expanded, ready to explode. He leaned forward and slapped repeatedly at Hatch's wrists.

You retarded—peeping up. You really are.

Cosmo smacked him again, short and sharp. He seemed to calm. And he leaned away from Hatch, slowly, and righted himself, his eyes minus their fierce light, and withdrew back into his empty fixed look. You shut up, or I'll give you some trouble.

Hatch lowered his hands. And if you do—

Cosmo readied his hand. Look out now.

Hatch guarded his head. He breathed like someone who had been running. He remembered the water pistol. Maybe if he had it now . . .

Cosmo lowered his hand. Touched the cord of his robe. Let's get this business outta the way.

Hatch could no longer feel the bear's teeth in his neck, but he knew it was there, still found it hard to move his legs, impossible to take his feet.

Cosmo moved back to the other side of the room, slippers clapping, and leaning so far forward that he might have fallen flat on his face. He entered the cone of light, turned, and faced Hatch. Spread his arms wide. Welcome brother—speaking with his new impenetrable expression.

Hatch rolled his hands over his chest, searching, certain that the bear was tired out from all of the struggle and activity and had gone into hibernation.

Cosmo squatted on his haunches, the low position propelling more air up into his rising black cheek. He fingered the sheet. Come over here behind this sheet.

I see you, Hatch said. Don't think I don't. But the bear had settled into a deep slumber, and his brother watched him, a fading glow, even dull radiance, some unclaimed and impatient skin shape summoned by dim regret—a singular desire to look deed and aftermath stonily in the face and move on.

Same

Boards don't hit back.
– BRUCE LEE

I

His mother's name was Glory Hope Lincoln. His father had a wandering eye. On a bright summer day, she cut his daddy's dick off and threw it out the window.

You dead, bitch, Daddy said.

The Lord giveth and he also taketh away, Glory said.

Daddy put his hands over his crotch and went searching for his member. Later, Glory and the cops found him slumped against a mailbox five blocks away.

The officers were all white men, Glory said, but they didn't arrest me. They knew that it was the Lord himself who had guided my hand. Oh, Jesus is a mighty man!

Glory always told the story to him, her son, Lincoln Roosevelt Lincoln, in the kitchen, a large room, hot and bright inside with sunlight from the big window behind the sink. She sat stiff in her chair—akin in structure and appearance to an infant's high chair, it was specially built to compensate for her height—her eyes closed, her head back, and her thick gray hair pulled tight into a ponytail, as if someone were trying to snatch her out the window. She was the darkest shade of black, and Lincoln wondered how she could be his mother, since he himself was so light that even a touch of sun made him tan. Her cheeks glowed red, two small furnaces—this woman round and fat from good living.

Lincoln sat in his own chair, tears hot on his cheeks.

Glory opened her eyes and looked him full in the face. Man, she said, don't lose your head over a piece of tail!

Lincoln could no longer remember when she had first told him the story, but when he was eight, she said, Set your tail down over there, where I can see you. He sat down in his chair.

In her black dress suit, she was small and motionless. Sunlight draped a shawl over her shoulders. She had closed her eyes, eased her head back, and told the story. Concluded thus:

Men should sow their oats, she said.

Yes, ma'am.

Then marry at thirty.

Yes, ma'am.

But men are heathens.

Lincoln had thought for a moment, sincere. Jesus was a man, he said.

Glory shot her eyes open. Brought her head forward and looked at Lincoln for a full minute, her face as still as a rock. Then she slapped him, hard. Water cascaded from his eyes. (Until the day before his death, he never cried again, not even in jest.) Glory went over to the sink and washed her hands, as if she had been dealing with something unclean. *You don't fuck with Jesus.*

Glory loved Jesus, the only man she ever cooked for, in a greasy ritual she performed once a year, on his birthday. Turkey and dressing, ham, fried gizzards, chitlins, hog head cheese, black-eyed peas, butter beans, neck bones, corn bread, buttermilk and side meats, candied yams, smothered chicken, collard greens, eggnog, and pecan pie. They would sit down to a table overgrown with a smoky jungle of plates.

Taste and see, Glory would say. Jesus is good.

They would eat their supper and afterward spend the evening before the fireplace in the living room, Glory singing: *Come by here Lord, come by here.*

Lincoln grew, so that by the time he was ten, Glory barely reached his shoulder. Whenever some thought thickened his mind, he would walk around the house wide-eyed like a baby. He could never do right for doing wrong, and Glory always found something suspicious in his look, so Lincoln began to develop the habit of beaming a golden smile at her, a ritual meant to comfort and ease but that over time altered the muscles in his face to such a degree that the corners of his mouth hurt. One day, as she sat tall in her high chair in the kitchen, and he in his chair, giving her his aching smile, he decided to question her about the central mystery in her life.

Mamma?

Yes?

Where my daddy?

I done told you a thousand times where your daddy at.

I know, but—

She jerked him up by the collar. You ain't been listen?

No, ma'am. He looked down into her face but avoided her eyes.

You must just be hardheaded?

His heart tightened at the hard threat of her question. No, ma'am.

What yo problem, then?

He framed his words. Where is my daddy Jesus?

The fire in Glory's cheeks cooled, but Lincoln could feel the heat from her smoldering eyes. Boy.

Yes, ma'am.

Listen carefully.

Yes, ma'am.

Jesus can see into the heart.

Yes, ma'am.

God gave me children as a token of his own suffering and love, and for my devotion to him.

Yes, ma'am.

His son saw into my heart.

Yes, ma'am.

Never close your heart to Jesus.

Yes, ma'am.

Glory was a woman of mean understanding. Burns covered her forearms, the blackest part of her body, and her fingernails were so black and her fingers so flat (old pone-pan hands, Lincoln called them in the full force of his anger) that she always wore gloves in public (and sometimes even when she ate) and long full dresses—even the sleeves long—that revealed no flesh. She walked slowly and carefully, like one just learning. Lincoln studied her through the keyhole of her bedroom door, observed that she slept with her eyes open, her body trembling at scenes of destruction and devastation, projected onto the ceiling and walls, that her eyes alone could see. Eyes that saw in clouds the shapes of disaster. Saw spirits wrestling in the sky and swift-winged angels zooming over the world. For her, ordinary language was an undecipherable hieroglyphics, and Lincoln had to sit before the warmth of the fireplace, where she knitted the same quilt she would finish only moments before her death, and read her the mail, or her favorite black newspaper, the *Black Star*, and magazine, *Mirror of Liberty*, or the printed labels on foodstuffs, tin cans, and cardboard boxes.

She would spend most of the day in the kitchen, reading the only written words she understood: those of the Bible. Then she would summon Lincoln to her company for conversation. Lincoln forever on hand at the pointed moment of memory and reflection, for how can progress be measured unless we reconstruct and reanimate the past? She said her say, Lincoln hearing but not always listening, until she circled back to the present, depleted, it would seem, from the telling. She would spend the remainder of the day knitting and humming before the fireplace.

One day, she called Lincoln into the kitchen. Boy.

Yes, ma'am.

Yellow niggers darken with age.

Ma'am?

But she left him with that piece of fact-threat-advice and went to bed singing:

> *Jesus loves me*
> *Yes I know*
> *Cause the Bible*
> *Tells me so.*

The baby was hunched into a heap, legs crooked, head touching knees. It's too damn hot in here, he thought. These days, you can't find peace anywhere.

Lincoln always rose at dawn, had done so for as long as he could remember. So too this day. It was warm and black and close under the covers. He raised himself slowly out of bed, fingered his penis (limp), moved over to the black drapes fronting the windows, and drew them open to a flood of light. Blinking, he stood looking out onto the city's skyline, a view he took pride in, his thirty-six-story-high penthouse perch scanning across the very heart of the city. Sunlight flamed about the roofs of buildings—tall brick and steel boxes blaring many-glassed reflections. He looked down onto the Eisenhower Expressway and saw cars moving on a sea of blacktop, wheels and engines silent. He could hear nothing of the outside. Somewhere behind him wood popped and hissed; he turned to see his bed, as high and thick as a mausoleum, glowing as if on fire, black sheets bright under the light, like the moonlit surface of water, spotted with two drops of semen, fallen stars on the rippling satin. His sight looped back to the window and skyline, and he gazed on in silence and kept looking, sunlight stroking his back in anxious anticipation. Blind fingers sought his penis and examined it. Erect.

Moving on, the next juncture of his morning routine required preparation of his bath—foam and bubbles, plenty of bubbles and foam. He lowered his body into the tub, enjoying the warm water and the clean soap smell. Some thirty minutes later—time formed and held in foam, time bouncing and echoing in every bubble—he stepped free of the tub and toweled his body dry, then made his way to the full-length mirror, leaving behind a soapy trail. He was tall, but of average build, since he never exercised. He believed that independence and hard work should be rewarded. If he sweated, he wanted to be paid.

Jesus fixed it so we won't never have to work, Glory said.

Yes, ma'am.

You ain't no slave.

Yes, ma'am.

Niggers shouldn't work for the white man. She mailed out anonymous donations to black businesses and instructed Lincoln in the art of writing chain letters—words are dreams—(a dollar enclosed in the envelope), which read: *Praise Jesus, you lucky so and so. Cast down your bucket where you are. Pass it on. Pass it on.*

Lincoln back-combed his fine curly hair into one thick pomaded wave. Polished his teeth and took time to evaluate the possibilities of his appearance. His eyes were his best feature: large, wet, and full of—his women believed—the tears of a sensitive masculinity. Sensitive teeth, sensitive stomach, he made his way to the kitchen—cool air playing over his naked body—where he breakfasted on powdered foods, the stuff of astronauts, then slipped into a white linen shirt and slacks fitted with a thin black leather belt. He removed a photograph that he had received several weeks earlier, from an Emmanuel Lead, who had written a letter on the back of the photograph in thick-tipped lasting black marker, from the black file cabinet next to his bed.

Dear Sir,

I entered the army because I come from a patriotic and Catholic family. Imagine, a black patriot and Catholic. Nevertheless, I wanted to be a career soldier. Reality changed many of my views, although I'm still a God-fearing Christian. Your work has helped me and many of the other brothers. We have hardened into one flame. We hold monthly discussions of your books and, in your honor, have started the General Black-Veteran Business Association. We also sell certificates of honorary African American citizenship to white soldiers. We've gotten some opposition from a few fire-eating racists who would put a black eye into our efforts. But we endure. After our release from active duty, we plan to start a guerrilla marketing firm. On behalf of the association, I thank you. Find here a picture of me and my beautiful wife, Frieda. It's our wedding picture. My Frieda and I love your books. We have read every one cover to cover and more than once.

P.S. Keep writing.

Lincoln studied the photograph, a glossy print showing a happy couple in a tropical setting. Emmanuel Lead stood tall and proud in his uniform, his forehead vast over deep-set and smoldering eyes, his black hair back-combed into a thick pomaded wave, his wife calmly beside him, the crown of her head level with his shoulder. Her features were blurred under a hard core of sunshine, her raised white veil the perfect setting for a rare jewel of a face—but empty, revealing nothing. A woman of substantial flesh and skin—wide-hipped and round-busted, enticing him to seize the moment by the throat and wonder if she might fit smoothly into his Monday slot and complete his life: six women for the six days of the week. (Sunday was his day of rest.)

Monday. The first of his last two mornings on earth. (Countdown: four, three—) He read the *Daily Observer.* (He had a subscription.)

The usual number of rapes, stabbings, and bodies bludgeoned beyond recognition. No other events caught his attention.

Tuesday. (—two, one. Change count.) And his thirtieth birthday. In the *Daily Observer* he read about a suicide of a former FBI informant who had infiltrated AAMM, the African American Men's Movement, a black nationalist and quasi-paramilitary organization, at the bureau's urging and with its support. He was survived by no one, and, though the article included no photograph, Lincoln had experienced nothing in his thirty years like the jolt he received from the man's name. Lincoln Jefferson Lincoln. His twin brother.

But before that, on that first last morning, the elevator doors wrapped him in steel gray and swept him down to the granite lobby. He stepped out of the building into a noisy collision of speech, shouts, and whistles: the sounds of the city. The sky was clear, the sun hot. Nothing but people, concrete, and steel in every direction. The wind shoved his back as he walked, but his pace grew slower with every step, metal-heavy sun burning down on his head. He touched his face and felt hot rubber. Melting.

Glory's stories and visions had spread like hot dirt over everything in his life. In his childhood, he would sit before the fireplace while Glory was in the kitchen, reading the Bible forward and backward through the red hate of his blood. She would enter the room and smile a broad glow of contentment. Seat herself before the fireplace. He would retire to his room, where he spent long hours of contemplation, jotting down ideas in a diary. Going there to know there, he started to write at length about everything that stabbed at him, recording every microscopic detail, for he wanted to expand the possible and unravel Glory's mystery. Steal the sacred fire and see inside his own life.

He had spent his adult years trying to verify the facts of Glory's crime but found no newspaper articles, no police reports, no witnesses. What was his father's name?—his birth certificate listed *J. Christ*—and where was his twin, Lincoln Jefferson Lincoln? A nameless father and a brother who existed only in name. Death was the starting point, but dead niggers tell no tales.

The day after Glory killed Lincoln's father, she discovered that she was several weeks pregnant with twins. She also learned that she had money in the bank, and plenty of it. (Insurance?) I was blessed with a triple miracle, she said. I wanted to share my good fortune with other colored folks. I put yo brother up for adoption. Then I moved from the third floor of that ole rundown building where we was living and into this good house in this good black neighborhood.

Glory was clean and neat and kept her low brick house and even concrete walkway clean and neat. Trees stretched their branches over a grassy lawn. Lincoln would walk in the yard, wind whipping the branches, and touch rough bark or the dry twigs of a hedge. He mowed the lawn and trimmed the bushes. This fine yard was fronted by a tall black wrought-iron fence. Here, Lincoln never allowed the images of the world to reach his heart. Forever vexed by questions he held in the full lens of his mind, burning, a clarifying hate swelling inside him that fueled new ideas and questions.

Though he hoped to shape his twenty-year diary of ponderings and reflections into a memoir, *The Autobiography of Black Life*, the last nine years had seen him produce nine novels about Henry "Hard Rock" Henson, the H-Man, a renegade black grunt in Vietnam. Hard Rock, Hard for short, lived a creed of illimitable ferocity. Hard knew the jungle like a private estate he had drafted and constructed. He would kill an officer (usually white) just as quickly as he would a gook. He greased his bullets with spit and spit with bullet force.

Though Lincoln had never seen the war, he had read dozens of books and articles about Vietnam. He wrote under the nom de plume the General, and his publishers marketed and promoted the novels as the fictionalized memoirs of a former high-ranking officer of the war who had to remain anonymous, for obvious reasons, offering in place of an author's dust-jacket portrait a stylized print showing a military uniform sprawled upon and crumpled across a bed like cast-off skin. Controversial and sure to sell in these times. And sell it did, the fire of Lincoln's words spreading throughout all of the major book clubs and finding an equally broad audience with servicemen and servicewomen in all branches of the military, who saw the General as a soldier's Ann Landers, Oprah Winfrey, or Miss Lonelyhearts. They wrote him volumes of letters about their most intimate problems. Once a week, Lincoln's publishers would forward him a sack or two of mail, and he would read each letter slowly and carefully, notepad and pen at the ready, logging important names, details, and events, compiling rap sheets and packets of data for future reference.

The previous week, Lincoln had received an anonymous letter informing him of Emmanuel's death. According to the letter, several white MPs had not taken kindly to the honorary certificates and demanded a stop. Emmanuel told them to kiss where the sun don't shine. The following day, the association found him floating in the swimming pool. His eyes had popped out of their sockets, but someone had bleached them clean of blood and tried to force them back in.

Lincoln had penned two chapters of his tenth novel, but a deep feeling told him that he would never complete it. He had in the back of his head a sense of impending punishment. Lately, he sensed something coming together in strangeness, something that only increased the hopeless gulf he felt between his past and his future. There was a stone on his chest and an even heavier stone deep inside him, weighing him down. And now, as he walked, he could hear the stones knock, could feel himself sinking, despite his strong body. Tomorrow he would be thirty, but his power to save himself had already faded from his muscles.

Reaching the corner, Lincoln looked at his watch. Eight thirty a.m. Unbeknownst to him, at that very moment another man, from the apartment complex five blocks south, committed suicide when *he* ran onto the Eisenhower Expressway and was struck by a Cleaning Magic diaper-service truck—a pilot without a flight plan, riding a rainbow's arc fifty feet above the expressway—in virtually the same spot where Lincoln would be struck the following morning. *Second morning, second truck.* The two men were strangers to one another, but the same womb had borne them both. It was only at the moment of his death that Lincoln Roosevelt Lincoln realized the conspiracy against him. Two men unaware, moving toward the same fate, in the same city. A spider retracting two threads into the center of its web.

Lincoln observed a traffic cop directing two phalanxes of moving steel, one northbound, the other southbound. Even from where he stood, Lincoln could tell that the cop's skin was rough, like a stone worn away by water. His uniform shone a navy blue and he held his head high, a cap on top. Lincoln moved closer, saw the cop's tiny buckshot eyes, heard a voice loud enough to wake the dead. The cop closed his eyes with every shout, carried away by deep emotion. Keep moving. Open. Keep moving. Shut. That's green, not greens. Don't stop to eat. That yellow ain't no chicken. That red ain't no wine, so don't you whine. So lucky God didn't make me a cabdriver.

At the next corner Lincoln saw a boy as tall as him, only leaner. Shoe shine, brother? the boy asked.

Lincoln accepted the offer.

The boy put black polish on the edges of his fingers, then moved his hands over Lincoln's cordovans, the pointed toes like weapons. Soon, the boy was slapping and rubbing a rag against them.

Brother, you know those white men are devils. He popped the rag.

Lincoln didn't say anything.

Bent over at the waist, the boy kept his legs locked straight, careful not to get any polish on his short-sleeve white dress shirt. He wore a black tie—snake-tongue thin—jeans, and Nike gym shoes. He had wonderfully clear skin, but his nose was pushed back into his face as if recoiling from some foul odor. So that no one might miss it, his body emitted the peculiar sweet and powdered smell of a baby.

Lincoln was about to enter the yard, when Glory called him.

See my hands? She removed her gloves.

Yes, ma'am.

I got frostbitten when I was a baby.

Yes, ma'am.

See these arms? She rolled up her sleeves.

Yes, ma'am.

I got burned when I was a baby.

Yes, ma'am. Lincoln pressed back into the squeezing dark of the hall, smiling to himself.

I may be short and fat, but I knows my wings gon fit me well.

Yes, ma'am.

He got a white robe for me.

Yes, ma'am.

He got me a seat up in the kingdom.

Yes, ma'am.

He got me a bed in the upper room.

Yes, ma'am.

I will walk on golden clouds, hand in hand with my Jesus. O flesh of my flesh!

Nothing but devils. The boy lifted his head and looked up into Lincoln's face, eyes bright with the memory of some deed.

They were standing on the corner of Congress Avenue, Lincoln facing the street, the steel wall of the Garden Tower Apartments behind him. He loved corners. Here, the world was going on, and he was there to perceive it.

What do you think of the white man?

The only white man Lincoln gave a damn about was Jesus, the Holy Redeemer, the man who had appeared to Glory in a dream. Chop off that nigger's dirty dick, Jesus said, and to thee all things shall be added.

Was Jesus a white man? Lincoln asked.

Yes, Glory said. Unless he's passing.

Glory hated white folks. God is black, she said. She sought out TV shows that featured white people being maimed or killed. She cheered every death, every gunshot. And whenever she watched news broadcasts and saw that a white person had died in a car accident or a plane crash or by falling glass, she would bow her head and say, Thank you, Jesus. Thank you. We are surely God's chosen people. At night, Lincoln heard her pray for God to put ground glass or spiders in every white person's buttermilk. He never discovered the actual source of her hatred, and at the time of her death, Jesus remained the only white man she liked.

Brother, what do you think about the white man?

I don't know, Lincoln said.

What? The boy scrunched up his face in disbelief. What?

Lincoln was tired of black folks blaming the white man for everything. Tired of them (us) marching and demonstrating and singing and shouting our lives away. White man this, white man that. Spilled milk, spoiled milk, injustices both real and imagined nothing more than specks of events and facts in the larger canvas of history. But why reveal his true feelings to this insignificant boy? Expression (communication) involves the monumental task of encounter.

I don't know, he said.

Cars zoomed past, coming and going, waves of noise and exhaust like an accumulation of ghostly presences heard and felt but unseen. People bunched together at the pedestrian crossing like herds of cattle. Others rushed about in all directions as if hurrying out of the rain. But the day was bright and the sun was high and Lincoln felt sun crawling on his face and arms, felt sun transforming him into some being of light and heat. The boy's nostrils cocked up at him, wide and deep, so much so that Lincoln imagined himself falling tragically inside them, lost forever.

As far as he knew, Glory was never sick a day in her life. The morning she gave up her spirit, she called him into her room. Her green shutters were thrown open to the world, sunlight pouring through the window and splattering the wall behind her bed, where she lay, her small head resting on a pillow, her magical quilt drawn up to her chin, as hot as it was, with only her two black hands and face outside it. Lincoln moved close to her side and saw wrinkles radiating out from the center of her nose, making her face look like a broken plate that had been pieced back together. A dim fire lit her cheeks.

I am bounding toward my God and my reward, she said.

Yes, ma'am.

Jesus will be calling you too someday.

Yes, ma'am.

She reminded him of the mason jars in the cellar, filled with quarters and half-dollars, the jewelry in the cookie jars under her bed, and the drawer with her burial policy, savings bonds, will, and lawyer's name and phone number.

You better mind your p's and q's, she said.

Yes, ma'am.

She looked at the ceiling. Lord, open up the gate. She closed her eyes, the fire in her cheeks simmering down then extinguishing. The room became a chamber of silence.

Free at last! Lincoln said, under his breath. He was nineteen and ready to see the other side of the shining coin.

That very morning, he tried to have her body cremated. This postmortem arrangement the will forbade—*see the stipulation printed in the next-to-the-last clause*—so, without the usual ritual and ceremony, he stuck her in the ground. Sold the house to the first buyer. Sold her magical quilt. For one dollar. Cash.

A swirl of violent life. Lincoln's face went hot and heavy. He leaned back against the wall, thrown, unmoored.

You all right, brother? Under the sun's glare, the boy squinted up at Lincoln, who rode waves of light and shadow, saw the boy moving in and out of focus, the crowd swaying this way and that. His lungs needed room to breathe, the street a cage of running motors and rushing feet. He felt hollow, something trembling deep in his stomach, so he shut his eyes and took a deep breath, but the air was thick and bitter in his mouth, and he could hear cars in the distance and smell their fumes. He coughed.

Hey, the boy said.

Lincoln heard the brush fall to the ground.

Don't cough on me.

Lincoln couldn't move or speak.

Damn!

But Lincoln was hollow. Body eaten by flames.

Coughing on people and shit.

The boy's voice came to Lincoln from a distance. Though his eyes were closed, Lincoln felt that everything about him was radiating, sun constricting his face and chest.

Germs. I might catch something. Shit.

Lincoln drew another deep breath, a sanitizing breeze that moved through his body and beat back the sickness. The free oxygen gave him enough strength to raise himself upright. He opened his eyes, looked at the boy from head to foot, slowly and deliberately.

The boy's face fell a little. Didn't mean no harm, he said.

Lincoln increased his look to full intensity.

You know I didn't mean no harm. It's just that white folks— Man, that's why we got all these problems. Anger shook the boy's thin frame. Motherfuck the white man!

Lincoln found himself looking into a face that had hardened into leather, a mouth now set in lines of hatred. The boy's pose did nothing to lessen his anger. He spoke through clenched teeth. How much do I owe you? He extended a five-dollar bill.

The boy looked at the bill. Five dollars, he said. He snatched the bill. That green counts. He was dead serious.

Lincoln had money in the bank and plenty to spread around. The profits from his books had surpassed his inheritance. No small achievement, for Glory had had substantial property—the house alone was a heap of bread—had had shares in everything from Standard Oil to Rough Rider Saddles.

Lincoln started toward the bus stop, buildings blazing bright in the hot shimmer of the sun. He walked as fast as his legs could carry him, the world on fire.

Fight the white man!

Lincoln didn't turn around. Moved with determined splashing strides. A billboard looming above the roof of the Walgreen's across the street read *Jesus Is Lord over Our City* beneath an illustration of a big white Jesus with one hand raised as if taking a vow, being sworn in, the other hand placed over his heart. But Lincoln did not slow his pace for a better look. He had a client to meet, Mrs. Frieda Lead. He didn't own a car. Public transportation afforded him the opportunity to study ordinary people firsthand. He quickened his step, shirt sticking to his skin as he moved under the torch of the sun.

He made it to the Metro stand just as the bus came grinding down the middle of Washington Boulevard. It banked sharply, brakes squealing. A decal taped to the windshield greeted all boarding passengers: a white hand and a black hand jointly holding the two ends of a red valentine heart, words penned in black letters across its center—*The Love Bus.*

The doors squeaked open. Step onto the Love Bus, the driver said. Lincoln boarded the vehicle and slipped a silver dollar into the fare box. The driver cut the bus into the center of the boulevard, throwing Lincoln's feet out from under him. He struggled to keep his balance.

Welcome to the Love Bus. At the sound of my voice, the time will be eight thirty-five.

Are you trying to be funny?

No, sir. Folks don't like to be late. Tall, almost a giant, the driver sat cramped down in his seat, leaning forward over the big steering wheel. Excluding his pop eyes, he was well built and handsome. About Lincoln's age.

You can get hurt that way, Lincoln said. He sat down in the seat perpendicular to the driver's.

And I can get hurt getting out of bed too, but that don't mean it's gon happen.

Lincoln's throat clogged with words. His whole body tightened.

The driver watched the traffic but held Lincoln in the corner of his eye.

You're a wise guy, Lincoln said.

Folks don't like to be late. I have a job to do.

Lincoln read the driver's nameplate: ULYSSES TUBMAN. I'll tell you what, Ulysses, Lincoln said.

The driver gave Lincoln a quick full look.

Don't talk to me, and I won't talk to you.

The driver tightened his grip on the steering wheel. God bless you, he said.

Lincoln noticed that the driver had propped one of his novels, *Hard Rock's Hole in One*, in the space between the windshield and dashboard, but Lincoln suppressed any glow of recognition. You're lucky I'm in a good mood today, he said.

God bless you, the driver said.

Stupid bastard. He scouted out the other passengers. Two girls sat a few seats behind the driver. The first day of spring found them in bicycle pants and sleeveless T-shirts, their skin like melted caramel under the sunlight. They wore the latest haircuts, one girl completely bald on the right side of her head, thick corn rolls trailing down the left, the other girl bald on her left, corn rolls on her right. An older woman sat a few seats behind them, sharp in a full-length black dress, with a prim white bow at the neck, stockings, and pumps. A sporty tam mushroomed above her head, white hair spilling out from under it like melting snow. *Granny, you must have been fine in your day.* A white man lay curled up in the seat at the rear of the bus, clutching the boomerang-shaped collar of his winter coat. *Some of these poor white trash are worse than the lowest niggers and all their low sorry ways.* Lincoln watched the two girls, every movement, every gesture.

Tall, skinny, and knock-kneed, twelve-year-old Mary lived a few houses down from Lincoln—a year older—in the John Henry Homes development, a tidy block of two-flat government housing projects with grass clean enough to eat. Lincoln tried to woo her with sugary gifts of Now and Laters, strawberry pop, barbecue potato chips, licorice, salted sunflower seeds. When this didn't work, he wrote her poems and letters in the solitude of his room. On a day when he found the courage, he followed her home from school, read snatches of red words.

Mary laughed and laughed. You so corny.

Another day, he pulled out his dick and shook it at her.

Ugh. You so nasty. She kissed him, working her tongue.

They rushed over to her house, since her parents were away laboring for bread and keep.

I don't want no baby, she said. She wriggled her dress down over her hips.

In the darkness of her room, the bed creaked and her moans crackled in Lincoln's ears. Perhaps his piston-rhythm piston weight was breaking and crushing her bones, but he didn't stop until he came. Holy Father! he shouted.

JEFFERY RENARD ALLEN

Ugh. You peeing in me, Mary said. She pushed him off her. Left the room and returned, lickety-split, with her German shepherd, a beast with teeth like jagged cliffs. Lincoln finished zipping his pants. Mary pointed at him. Frankenstein, sic! But Lincoln had already started for the door. He proved faster than the dog.

Lincoln could still feel Mary's kiss burning on his lips.

Cool air blew through the bus, which had taken on a little speed, tires humming. Frieda Lead lived in Crescent Hills, at the very end of the boulevard, an interracial suburb with smoothly paved streets, gravel drives, trees on low hills, mowed lawns, and trimmed hedges. The bus traveled a perfect loop, so that, later, Lincoln had only to cross to the other side of the boulevard for the return ride home.

Niece, did you see what was on the flo of the bathroom yesterday? the first girl said.

Um-huh. Girl, who would leave something like that on the flo? the second girl replied.

The white man came from the back of the bus with a funny little walk: one shoulder down, then the other, hands stuffed in the pockets of his winter coat. The old woman pinched her nose as he passed. He sat down in the seat directly behind the first girl, who was closest to the aisle. Both girls spun in their seats.

Whatever was on that floor, the white man said, couldn't have been as ugly as your goddamn face.

Who you talkin to, gray? the first girl said.

I'm talkin to you, bitch!

Ut-oh, Niece. I'm gon cut this mudda fudda! She rose with switchblade swiftness and reached for something in the back pocket of her bicycle pants.

Nancy, be cool!

Lincoln bounded out of his seat and seized the girl's hand. It was hot. And soft. Take it easy, ma'am.

She tried to twist free of his grip. Let me go.

Please, ma'am. He's not worth it. Her skin was soft. And hot.

You better let me go. Nobody calls me a bitch.

He right, Nancy. Be cool.

He's not worth it.

Fuck you! the white man said to Lincoln.

Lincoln glared at him. He reeked of sweat, his hair matted like wet fur. He wasn't as old as Lincoln had thought; in fact, they could have been the same age. Fine skin fleshed out a face where green eyes shone through dirt like exotic gems. I suggest you find another seat, Lincoln said. He released the girl's wrist but held her in the corner of his eye.

The white man sprang to his feet, like ice water had been spilled on his back. He was small but solid. As he and Lincoln squared off, his face grew hard, eyes flooding, changing color, two pools of swirling blood.

Find a seat or I'll knock you into one, Lincoln said. He was on the edge of a great venture. He would leap over the gulf in his life.

Come on. The white man crouched low and raised his fists.

Lincoln showed him two sets of hard knuckles. I think you'd better get off the bus.

The white man maintained his crouch. Lincoln squeezed his fist and cracked his knuckles, mimicking the terrifying sound of some powerful force crushing steel. The white man pulled himself upright, fists raised. I'll fight you, he said, even though you ain't my size. Lincoln moved forward. The white man pop-locked in fear and fled to the rear exit of the bus. Leave me alone or I'll jump, he said. Lincoln took a step toward him. He jumped.

Gawd, Nancy said. You see that crazy white fool?

Um-huh, Niece said.

The bus screeched to a halt, throwing everyone forward. Lincoln regained his balance and walked with the slow certainty of a meter maid to the rear exit, where he stepped into the jumper's ghostly residue, thick stink. The near-giant driver came down the aisle, head bent to avoid hitting the roof of the bus. He looked at Lincoln, pop eyes swelling in anger. What the fuck is going on back here?

The old woman looked at Lincoln. He forced a paying passenger to jump from the bus, she said. The wrinkles in her face twitched like live wires.

Nawl, that white fool jumped from the bus, Nancy said.

My God! the driver said. He rushed to the rear exit, shoving Lincoln aside.

Yeah, Niece said. He called her a bitch, and this dude—she pointed at Lincoln—came back here to see what the deal was. The driver had already exited the bus.

Why don't you just shut your mouth, the woman said.

Make me. You ain't my mamma.

True, but I'll still slap the shit out of you.

Niece didn't say anything. Neither did Nancy.

Lincoln moved to a window. A crowd had gathered. The driver stood over the white man, who lay crumpled in the street.

I'm hurt, the white man said.

Right, the driver said.

I'm hurt!

The driver looked at him. I'll give you some hurt, he said. The wind moved over his shirt and the shirt over his muscles.

Okay, okay, the white man said. Help me up! He extended his arms, and the driver pulled him to his feet—an acrobatic routine. Easy, brother, the white man said. The driver gave him a look. Using both hands, he brushed the white man's coat free of dust, and the lucky recipient responded like some grim clown by snapping the creases in the driver's pants. The driver gave him a look. Then the white man spotted Lincoln and gave him the finger. The driver shoved the white man forward. Get on the bus. They forced a path through the crowd, dust clouds whirling behind them, and got back on the bus. The white man sat down in Lincoln's vacated seat, cuts, welts, and red half-moons mapping his face.

Hear ye, hear ye, the driver said. At the sound of my voice the time will be eight forty-five. Welcome to the Love Bus.

That scanlous white man, Nancy said.

Shit, Niece said.

Lincoln was heading directly for the white man when he spotted one of his novels, *Hot Nights and Napalm*, on Nancy's lap.

Excuse me, ma'am, Lincoln said.

What you want? She was still angry.

Let me introduce myself, ma'am.

Why bother.

Nancy, you need to quit.

I didn't catch your name, ma'am.

Why don't you go catch a truck.

Niece snickered.

You fast gals can get hurt talking to me like that, Lincoln said.

Mister, you better sit down, the old woman under the tam said. She had her hand on something bulging inside her purse.

Ain't gon be no mo shit on my bus! the driver screamed. He was watching Lincoln in his rearview mirror, pop eyes straining like water-filled balloons. Either you find a seat, or I'm callin the police.

You have a witness in me, the old woman said. My name is Barbara Bleach Breedlove.

Okay, the driver said.

That's Barbara Bleach Breedlove.

Lincoln gave her his meanest look.

Sir, you better keep your eyes where they belong.

I'm not bothering you, granny.

And you better watch how you speak to me, or I'll come over there and beat you like a bald-headed stepchild.

Lincoln spit out a laugh.

Okay now, the driver said.

Lincoln didn't want any trouble. The driver might be every bit as powerful as he was ugly. He slipped forward and took the seat at the rear of the bus. Felt something cold settle in his stomach.

It's been a pleasure doing business with you, the old woman said.

Amused, the driver shook his head.

The girls snickered, their shaved-braided heads moving as one. Lincoln just sat there. The white man winked a green eye at him.

Smirking and grinning, the girls exited the bus at the James Madison Public Academy. Lincoln noticed that Niece was also carrying one of his novels—spread the news: three sightings in less than an hour, in one location—*Brave and Tender*.

A few blocks later, the old woman rose to exit. She looked at Lincoln. Didn't nobody learn you nothing?

Well, granny, you sure didn't.

Just one more word, the driver said. He watched Lincoln in the mirror.

Lord, give me the strength so I won't have to hurt nobody today. The old lady's hair was so white under the sun that Lincoln's eyes began to hurt. *Old-ass granny*. She adjusted her white bow and rolled her own eyes at him as she exited. The white man went behind her. Brother, you have some ugly shoes, he said. He gave Lincoln the finger. *White trash*. Lincoln sat in silence.

The bus hummed to the bridge that separated Crescent Hills from the city proper. Lincoln saw rippling water beneath. Little by little, his death took shape. This morning, he would seduce Frieda Lead—*We're in this together, ma'am, you and me, the same*—then catch the bus back to the city. Under the lingering sweetness of his conquest, he would swagger down Congress Avenue. See the traffic cop again. At a chain bookstore he would purchase a copy of Judy Chicago's *The Dinner Party*. Once home, he would disrobe and retire to his bedroom to make careful study of the book's glossy and finely reproduced illustrations of postmodern vaginas. It would take him some time to emerge from this papery maze, satisfied and at ease with his discoveries. He would record the day's events in his diary—*Frieda Lead: she moved me*—work on his new novel, with little success, then go out for a walk and chance upon a flyer circulated by FUSION. Deck a white boy. Chase the speeding boy down Washington Boulevard. (His smell lingering. Jet trail. *Never seen anyone run so fast.*) Chance upon the billboard Jesus for the second time that day. See Jesus shake his head. Return home in the last shimmer of day. (Lamps already lit along the alleyways.) Receive an anonymous phone call: Brother, your days are numbered. The next morning, he would read the *Daily Observer,* see his brother's name, rush into the elevator and out the building onto the expressway. Never before had the sun shone so bright.

II

Frieda Lead lived in a small range house with a big picture window, like all the others extending along both sides of the street. Lincoln stood for a moment where her lawn began, observing the house, sun falling hot and bright on his face. Only then did he come to note that his skin had completely tanned. Several quick steps carried him forward. Walked up three short brick steps and pressed the doorbell, then stood waiting in the cool shade of the porch. His damp shirt set him to worrying, kicked up that rare emotion, fear. *What if I stink?* He waited a few more seconds, pressed the buzzer again.

Who is it?

Mrs. Lead? Mrs. Frieda Lead?

Yes?

Sorry to disturb you, ma'am. But I'm here on urgent business.

Who?

I need to talk to you about your husband.

What?

I am the General.

What?

I'm here on urgent business relating to your husband.

No response.

Mrs. Lead? He heard fingers at the peephole on the other side of the door. Ma'am?

Yes?

I must talk with you about your husband.

Are you a reporter?

No, ma'am. A friend.

There followed a long moment of silence.

Ma'am? He heard her fingers turning the locks. She opened the door, the chain still on, and stuck her face in the crack. What's this about?

I think I should speak to you inside, ma'am, in private. He looked around as if he were being followed. No other presence, nothing but the light, glare.

Another moment of silence, of watching and waiting.

My husband?

Yes, ma'am.

You're the author?

Yes, ma'am. If you'll allow me to explain. He placed the wedding photograph her husband had sent him where she could see it.

She shut the door, released the chain, then threw the door wide open. Please come in.

Thank you, ma'am. Inside it was cool and dark. I'm sorry if I upset you.

She took him by the elbow and led him to the couch. They both sat down. She took the photograph.

He wrote something on the back of it, ma'am.

She flipped it over and read the letter, then looked casually at Lincoln.

Yes, ma'am. He sent it to me.

I'll always recognize his handwriting. Emmanuel dotted his *t*'s.
She was silent for a moment, studying the letter. Good Lord, I'm
forgetting my manners. Can I get you some breakfast?

No, thank you, ma'am. But I will take a glass of water. The new
and dimmer setting had yet to cool his skin.

I'll get you a glass. She placed the photograph on the coffee table
in front of them.

Thank you, ma'am. Eyes still aching from the glare outside, he
was unable to see clearly—Frieda a blur that rose from the couch
and left the room—having only enough vision to take in and ad-
mire her healthy behind. He noticed a copy of the wedding picture
framed in oak on the table. He continued to look about, could just
make out the face of a white Jesus on the wall. That much certain.

Holy Father, Lincoln began, are you interested in my salvation?

What's that?

Lincoln hadn't heard her enter. She set the glass of water on the
table before him and sat down at one end of the sofa, he at the other,
but it was a small sofa, and they were sitting close.

I was speaking to the Holy Father, ma'am.

Praise Jesus, she said.

Praise Jesus, Lincoln said. He looked at the framed photograph.
You have my condolences. He drank the water in two rhythmic
gulps. It was cool and clean.

Would you like another glass?

If it's not a bother, ma'am.

No bother.

He watched the rough movements of her hips as she rose, her
behind round and fat the way he liked. She returned with another
glass.

We read all your books. She motioned to a bookcase in the corner. Every one. More than once.

My deepest thanks for the support.

Your ability to move people with words. Your feeling and understanding.

Nothing special. The rewards of hard work.

You are blessed. Jesus got his eye on you. Frieda went over to the case and removed a book, a hard-spined copy of the General's last novel, *Hard in Heaven*, which she held before Lincoln's face, opened to the title page, like a waiter at an upscale restaurant proudly presenting the menu.

I would be honored, ma'am. Lincoln removed a pen from his pants pocket, took the book from her, and autographed it: *To my true friend Frieda, with love and admiration. The General.* He wrote the exact date under the signature and returned the book to her.

She took a moment to read the inscription. You are so kind, she said. She met his eyes—hers round and puffy—and turned away.

My pleasure, ma'am.

She placed the book on the table, before the wedding photograph, then returned to her seat on the couch next to Lincoln. You look much younger than we imagined.

Lincoln smoothed the fold in his trousers. I keep in shape. But I suppose it's in the genes.

Her face was ordinary except for overly round cheeks that pulled her mouth into a permanent smile. And her eyes, swollen with grief, shone like black reflectors. She wore a short dress that fit tight across her firm outstanding breasts. Lincoln had to admit, Emmanuel had lived well. Oh yes. She placed her hands across her bare knees like napkins and picked up the photograph. He was a credit to the race and all good Christians, ma'am.

Thank you. She ran a hand down her face as if clearing her eyes of water. A knife of sunlight slashed through the space where the draperies met.

I'm sorry that I didn't know him better.

You knew Emmanuel?

Yes, ma'am.

He never told me.

We were part of an association, Lincoln said. Such lies were routine, in accordance with the dictates of his methods and plans, as he had a store of talk for each of his women. An association created by and for black veterans. A mutual-aid society.

Oh, the association. Emmanuel never told me that you were a member.

We keep our membership secret. But here—he reached into his pocket—I have this for you. He gave her a check for one hundred dollars.

Frieda took the check. What's this?

I'll bring one by every Monday.

But why?

It's our way of taking care of our own, ma'am. I'm here to assist you in any way I can.

Her legs showed beneath her skirt, but he always went slow with his women.

I don't understand.

God knows best, he said.

Praise Jesus.

Praise Jesus.

She cried—her head was small and round and heavy on his shoulder, and her tears were hot and wet—and so did he, forcing out actual tears. He showered her with innocent hugs and kisses. *Go slow, bro.*

Then they prayed. She had a special space for this purpose, a room—a walk-in closet—small and empty except for a wooden card table with a white candle on top. A four-foot-long Jesus hung suspended from the wall, a crown mashed down on his forehead, blood running in thick streams over his face, and his chest open like a door where a fat red heart bulged out. They kneeled before the table and bowed their heads before Jesus. Frieda prayed with the round beads of her rosary, over and over again. And as he prayed alongside her, Lincoln had a distinct feeling that someone was peeking out at him from the corner behind Jesus' heart.

They returned to the living room. Lincoln collapsed on the couch, Frieda beside him.

The baby bobbed on the cold water. He knew no strokes, only the dead man's float. Soon, he tired of it and, in cold dignity, raised his hands above the water. He had fine surgeon's fingers.

When Lincoln came to, Frieda was wiping his face with a wet rag.

Are you okay?

Yes, ma'am. The cords in his throat were tight. I'm sensitive to the heat.

Would you like some water?

Yes.

She exited the room. *Thank God for hips.* Jesus hung, silent, in the shadows.

O Holy Father, speak to me, Lincoln said.

What's that?

He hadn't heard her enter.

I was just seeking strength from the Redeemer.

Frieda set the glass of water on the table, between the two photographs. Should we pray some more?

In a little while, Lincoln said. He drained the glass, coolness sloshing around inside him.

You have great shoes, Frieda said.

Thank you.

They sat for a while, Frieda bumping his knee with hers at random intervals, a knee stinging with warmth. Lincoln looked her full in the face. She met his eyes for as long as he wanted. He gave her his best smile.

He left her house several hours later, she propped in the doorway, looking after him as they said their final good-byes. The day diminishing, manageable light. He blew her a kiss from that spot near the lawn where he had taken his first glimpse of her house.

Washington Boulevard. Lincoln felt a welling in his chest, a live coal, a wave of hurt spreading over his body. He rested for a moment against the rough brick face of a building. Some ten feet away a white boy was handing out flyers to passersby. He was as tall as Lincoln but rail thin, like a sheep shorn of wool, his gray eyes penetrating metal rods. A gold earring hung in orbit beneath his left earlobe, a bright miniature sun. And he was dressed street snazzy, in a black sweat suit, Nike sneakers, and a red baseball cap pushed way back on his head. He pivoted this way and that, shoving the flyers into any chest that chanced near him, all the while rapping some popular tune:

> *I'm smooth as silk and sweet as honey*
> *My fingers produce a lot of jam and money.*

He smelled so sweet that Lincoln wondered if his body were a chamber where, deep inside, incense smoldered and burned. Lincoln eased himself upright and took one of the flyers, then read the message printed there in bright shocking colors:

> *Know this title,* Hard In Heaven. *Authored by the General.*
> *This book sucks rank dick. A public-service message. FUSION*

Lincoln punched the white boy in the jaw, knocking him flat to the concrete, flyers spilling around him. What the fuck is this? The boy lay there, flat. Lincoln repeated his question. After a while, the boy managed to raise his head. Did you make this? Lincoln held the crumpled flyer in his hand.

The boy rested on one elbow, rubbing his jaw. Damn, homey, he said. You didn't have to fire on me. One side of his face was red.

Did you make this?

Goddamn. The boy rubbed his jaw.

Lincoln took a step forward. Did you make this?

No, don't hit me again. He made a pleading gesture with his hands.

Well, tell me. Did you make this flyer?

No.

Who did?

The boy rose to his knees. Took his time answering. The people I work for. He stood up, legs shaky. Tucked the flyers under his arm.

Who do you work for?

Man, those are some cool shoes. He studied Lincoln's pointed cordovans. Where did you cop them?

Look—

You must not do a lot of walking. The white boy stood there, rubber-legged.

Look, I'm going to ask you one last time. Lincoln was choking with rage. Who do you work for? He looked at the flyer. FUSION?

The boy shook his legs out.

Is it FUSION? Who do you work for?

Your mamma.

Holding Pattern

You always be seein some wacky shit on the train. Bitch slap a nigga for eyein her. Nigga piss on somebody who piss him off. Somebody get they throat slit over a gold chain. Shit like that. Like, this one time, I see this nigga fall flat on his back in the aisle. His teeth start rattlin like keys, and then he start shakin down the aisle and shake all the way to the other end of the car. Another time, this bitch face bleed away. I mean, she just sittin in her seat, mindin her own business, when this gash open in the sidea her neck. She put her palm over the gash, but it keep inchin up her neck. She put her other palm over that gash, but another gash start up the other sidea her neck. And these two gashes keep climbin and climbin, like they runnin a race, climbin right on up to her chin, up her face, then spread this net of blood all over her forehead. Bitch open her mouth like she fin to holler, but her tongue all red and drownin in blood. She put her hands over her face, and her hands change to blood. Then her head fall right offa her neck and go bouncin and rollin down the aisle. You shoulda seen it. Everybody screamin, tryin to jump off the train, wit nowhere to go. Some wacky shit.

The kinda shit this trippy world can put on your brain. And that ain't the least of it. You've heard about the jumpers, the suicides. Well, one time, I was all the way up inna first car, standin there lookin through the head window down on the tracks, seein what the engineer sees. And I see this lady kneelin between the tracks, inna path of the train. She looks up and sees the train bearin down on her. Her eyes get all wide and bright, and she gets that look like, Oh shit, what the fuck am I doin? So she hops up real quick and tries to squeeze her body flat against the tunnel wall so the train will slip right by her. But inna situation like that, you jus can't slim up and disappear.

Some trippy shit. And I could tell you more. Lots more. But to spare you the trouble, I'm jus gon tell you bout this one day that beat all. Why I had to stop ridin the trains altogether and institute a career change.

See, I had this routine. Rise early, freshen up. In this profession it's real important to smell good. For extra protection, smear some liquid soap under yo armpits. (This one department sto downtown got the best shit. That perfumey shit. Top-of-the-line. Always fill you up a lil plastic bag or two for later use.) That day I tiptoe down the fire escape (my landlord can be a real bitch when it's that time of the month) and make my way down to the cage for the mornin bets.

It's bright and early in the mornin, but niggas is already out. Standin on the sidelines around the cage, lookin through the metal fence, twenty foot tall or higher. Lined up like a flock of birds on a telephone wire. Don't play no ball myself. Niggas is too rough, all elbows and feet and teeth. But I don't mind watchin from the sideline. Place my bets and flip some money. I got a good eye for that kind of thing.

So, I'm bout to place my bet, when I see buck-wild Shiheed standin to my left, frownin all up inna my face. Shiheed, he one funny-lookin motherfucker. Long square bread-loaf head. Eyes all slanted like bird wings. Low eyes, low, almost sittin on his nose. Nostrils big enough to drive two Mack trucks through, cargo and all. Boogers big as peanuts. And these big white wide bright teeth like bars of soap. One other thing. This nigga is skinny. You can see his bones through his clothes. Skin thin as a kite. Pea, he say, I know you ain't bout to bet on that bitch-ass nigga.

I seen him play befo.

He won?

Yep.

That musta been his twin. Nigga be out here twenty-fo-seven gettin his ass toe up.

Really?

I kid you not. Look at him.

I look at him, but I can't see what I'm lookin at cause Shiheed got me all confused. So I think about it for a minute. Well, I guess you should know.

Of course. I'm out here all day.

So I bet on the other guy. We stand and watch the game. Do I need to tell you what happened? That bitch-ass nigga won.

Damn, Shiheed, why you fuck me up like that?

What? Nigga, who you tryin to blame? I'm tryin to look out for you.

Shit. You know how much that fucked me up?

Stop cryin. I lost money too, but you don't see me whinin like a bitch.

Shit.

You need to squash all that. I'm sorry. Truly. Sorry.

Fuck.

Why don't you place another bet.

Fuck that.

I understand. I owe you. Let me hook you up.

Man—

What can I get you?

I'm straight.

I got that powerful shit, that Mount Everest shit. Turn you into a superhero. Leap buildins in a single bound.

I'm on the clock.

Make time fly.

Really. I'm straight.

I heard that. My nigga. Make that money.

That's what I came to see you about.

What?

That thing I asked you to do fo me. A week before, I'd given Shiheed some ends to flip. Would you have a return on my investment?

Shiheed, he turns toward me, he puts his eyes on me. And they fix me like lasers, burn a hole right through my fohead. All these pictures of fucked-up bodies and piles and piles of dead niggas come flyin and screamin through that hole.

Not today. Things is slow.

I'm lookin at him, but I don't say anything.

But, hey, I'm gon hook you up.

I don't say anything. Ain't shit I can say.

You know I'm a man of my word. Catch me tomorrow.

Okay. Whatever you say.

My nigga. Hey, walk me up the block.

I really need to bounce.

I'm just goin up to the corner sto.

I got all this business I need to—

Damn, nigga. Why you trippin? You can't walk me up the block?

My skin shrink around my body, tight, beef jerky. Crazy motherfucker. Aw aight, I say. No problem, I say. I start to walk with Shiheed. Walk *behind* him.

You hear all that corny shit about the shadow of death followin somebody. Things you hear be true sometimes. Shiheed, he got one foot in prison, the other in the grave. I always walk a little behind him. Make sure I keep my eyes on that shadow. Keep that shadow between me and him.

Damn, Pea, he say. What the fuck is wrong wit you? Can't you walk like normal people?

I'm tryin to, I say. I got this condition.

Fuck yo condition. Shiheed's back pockets are packed full, bulgin out like two square titties. That condition wouldn be fear?

Ah, Shiheed. You know me.

Thought I did. So, you got my back?

Of course. But, hey, I ain't down wit that gangsta shit.

Nigga, there you go again. Trippin.

All I'm sayin—

Did I ask anything from you?

Look, I can't do no time. They'll break a lil nigga like me.

What? Nigga, you better wise up. Grow some hair on yo chest.

Just then we arrive at the sto.

You don't even know what I'm gon ask you.

I know. But thanks for the offer. I'll holla. I start to walk away.

Pea, you ain't gon come in the sto wit me?

Like I told you, I got to handle—

Nigga, you on some real fucked-up shit. Come on in the sto. Let me buy you a double ounce of courage.

I try to laugh it off.

Shiheed's face loosen up and he pop into his weird laugh. Nigga, you know I'm jus fuckin wit you. We cool?

Always.

My nigga. Shiheed stroll on into the sto.

Seein that he holdin out on my money—what I'm gon do, gat the motherfucker?—figure I haf to pull me some ends befo my afternoon hustle. So I bounce up to the El platform and wait for the train. I see this other head standin on the platform, a tall skinny nigga wit this green bandanna tied round his noggin, the knotted ends curlin out from his fohead. Nigga standin way high on his toes, head cocked back, like somebody tryin to snatch him into the sky. He see me and nod, all silentlike. I nod back. Then he go, It's a good day to make some money, if the squares don't get in yo way. He watchin me hard, real hard. So I walk to the other end of the platform.

When the train come, I hop on nice and quick and whip out my tall-boy malt-liquor can, papered over wit a black label wit red letters sayin UPLIFT CAREER ARTS ACADEMY. I make my way from car to car, holdin up my can and askin for donations. Most people ignore me, keep readin or talkin or starin outta the window. I can say I'm disappointed but can't say I'm surprised. That is one weak hustle. Always is. So I decide to resort to some real criminal behavior. I'm small and quick, and I can spot an expensive handbag from four car lengths away. Caiman, that is. That's the only thing I fuck wit. Don't even go after all that designer and name-brand shit. Everybody got that fake shit nowdays, so it's hard to tell. And another thing: all that fake-ass jewelry. So it's either the caiman or the money, the money or the caiman. I walk from car to car, fix people in my head and eyes as I pass, lookin for an easy mark.

I snatch this big fat bitch purse and she snatch back her purse, and me with it. Then she hop up from her seat and pimp slap me. Knock pain in my head. My brain hummin and vibratin like a dunked-on hoop rim. Bitch put me in this headlock and start squeezin my neck so hard that tears pop outta my eyes. Can't help but smell her underarms, right? People usually be stinkin under they arms, specially fat people. But this fat bitch bout the best thing I ever smelt. Smell like my whole head inna can fulla sweet flowers and fruits and candies. (She must know that department sto downtown.) But she don't give my nose long to appreciate. She take off her shoe—and she ain't got on no stockins—and I see the prettiest big toe I ever seen, no corns or nothin. Like a fine little titty. I'm watchin that titty when that fat bitch start hittin me upside the head with her hard-ass heel. Then she haul off and sling me away from her, a Rollerball move, and I feel sumpin twist in my neck, certain that this bitch done snapped my head off, that my head back there under her fine-smellin arm. I touch my head to make sure it's still there, and that's when I feel what I think is blood crawlin real slow down from the toppa my head. And I feel

JEFFERY RENARD ALLEN

this thing inside my head movin up and down like wings, wings flappin heavy and hard.

Fat bitch jus stand there lookin at me. She got all this white makeup on her face. Look like she dead. She be like, I'm tired of you lowlife niggers. Some people should never be born. Then that fat bitch kick me right in the nuts. Wit that fine-ass big toe.

You can make yo best money down in the financial district at lunchtime, when all the suckas spill outta they offices, hungry and loud. When you see a sucka, stick out yo belly and put on a sad face. Then you be like, Sir (or Madam), could you spare me a quarter for sumpin to eat? You can gank a few. And you can pull a big draw if you can find a whole gang of suckas from the same office all bunched up together.

Hunger make people feel all guilty and shit. An easy hustle. You can pull some substantial loot if it ain't too many bums around. I don't believe in knockin nobody's hustle, but a bum ain't nothin but a raggedy-ass scarecrow scarin all the money away.

Lucky for me, I see jus these two bums. One curled up off by himself inna space between two buildins, his face all red and shiny, set like a diamond in his grimy rags. And this other one, wearin a sign round his neck sayin INSULT ME FOR A DOLLAR. He jus sittin there on the dirty ground with his legs all folded Buddha-style, sittin there like he can't move, like his sign heavy as a concrete slab. Scarecrow.

I try not to sweat them bums, and start workin my hustle like I always do, but, for whatever reason, suckas is cheap today. I'm talkin nickels and dimes and pennies cheap.

I'm like, What the fuck is this, a recession or some shit? Gots to try another strategy.

So I see this one square, an easy mark, and I tell him that I'm wit the circus, the Man of Steel, and ask him if he wanna punch me inna stomach for a dolla. I pull up my shirt and brace myself. This square, he just look at me and shit. But that ain't all. Guess what he does next? Punk motherfucker spit on me. You heard me? Word. Yo, I'm all hot inside, hot, real hot. I'm like, Hey, money. Suck my dick. Then I run. Fast.

I use some of my draw for carfare and catch the train to my girl Juicy's crib. Juicy meet me inna hall with a kiss, all sexy and fly in this negligee, thin like a spiderweb. She be like, Hey, Pea, you sweet bitch. How you doin?

I had better days.

Poor baby. She takes my hand, turns—she got more ass than a donkey; I ain't gon tell you bout her face—and leads me into her crib. Then she leave me standin in the middle of the room and go over and sit down on the couch in fronta the TV to watch her favorite talk show—You know this my show—all content wit her snack: root beer and potato chips wit hot sauce. She be like, Pea, I was gon give you some. But, damn, I'm sick.

What's wrong?

My throat sore. I been smokin trees all day, but it don't do nothing.

Oh, I see. Kids ain't ready?

No. Ain't you hear me? I'm sick.

Sorry.

What? she say. Sorry? She frown up her face. What *sorry* gon do fo me? Can't you order me a pizza or sumpin? Some Chinese food? Home delivery?

I got to make them ends first. We got this sweet business arrangement, my after-school hustle. I give her twenty-five dollars a day for the use of her sons, Crust and Hamfat. Fifteen dollars for the older one. He ten. And ten dollars for the younger. He seven. Suckas like kids. On good days, I can turn a nice lil profit. On bad days, I'm lucky to break even.

Aw ight. Well, you better go get them boys, then.

I go into the bedroom, where Crust and Hamfat all holed up

wit the Nintendo game at the foot of the bed, lookin up at the TV on the stand above them. What up, yall?

What up, Pea.

What up.

Ready to make that money?

Can we finish our game first?

Yeah. I'm whoopin his ass.

You wish.

Come on, fellas. Time is money.

Ahhh.

I take them back out into the other room. Juicy look up at me from the couch. Yall ready? We nod. Hold up. I'll walk yall to the train. She goes in the bedroom. I take the time alone with the kids for a last-minute review.

You got the wig?

Yeah.

And the dress?

Yeah.

And you practiced the rhyme?

Yeah.

Let me hear it.

Do we have to?

I don't feel like it.

Aw ight. Stop whinin. But you better not mess up.

Juicy come outta the room stylin some stupid gear. This leather top all tight over her titties. These little shorts, real tight too. And some sandals, toes stickin out like a turtle inside his shell, each toe-nail painted a different color. Aw ight, yall. Let's go.

So we bounce from her crib and head for the El, Juicy hangin all on my arm, though she taller than me, the kids holdin hands in fronta us. The hood gnats see me and start wavin their wine bottles, glass flags. They swarm over and start in wit the beggin. Look at the happy family. I got a family too. Aw, Pea, you a righteous brother.

Can't you set me straight? Family man, let me hold a ten to run up and see my PO. Can't you let me hold five till Thursday? I'm good for it. I'll pay you on Tuesday fo a taste today.

Hey, Juicy say, step the fuck off. What do we look like, the Red Cross or some shit? Those niggas quiet down and disappear like roaches into dark cracks. Then Juicy turn to me. She be like, Pea, I know you don't be givin them broke niggas no money. I turn my face away. You better not. A nigga will ride yo jock worse than a bitch.

We go on a ways. What time you think yall be back?

Not too late.

Pick me up a pack of cigarettes. I'll pay you back.

I don't say nothing.

Be careful wit Ham. He got a slight cold. Now, yall mind Pea.

Yes, ma'am.

I don't wanna hear bout yall actin up.

We ain't. We gon be good.

Some big fat sloppy motherfucker is comin up the block toward us, hoggin the street. I curve around a lamp pole to keep from runnin into him.

Damn, Pea, Juicy says. What the fuck is wrong wit you? Ain't I told you bout splittin poles? Bad luck.

But that dude—

I can't have you cursin no bad luck on my sons.

You believe in all that?

She looks at me. Is you stupid or what?

I turn my face away. A cage is a little ways up, and as we pass by, who do I see on the other sidea the fence, watchin the game? Shiheed. Shit. Shiheed and Juicy hate each other, cause Juicy is mouth dangerous and Shiheed'll slap a bitch inna minute. Shiheed looks over and catches my eye. I turn my head. Too late.

Yo, Pea. What the deal, son?

He walks over, stands lookin at me through the diamond spaces of the fence. I keep walkin, but he follows us along the fence, Juicy inches from him.

Nigga, what you doin up here? Shiheed don't even look at Juicy.

You know, doin my—

I know you ain't hangin now wit them project niggas.

I feel quick heat on my skin.

Got way too much pride for that. You handle that business?

Yep.

My nigga. Pea. Always doin yo thing. You still doin that thing, right?

You know me.

Yeah, I know you. Shiheed sucked his teeth.

Then Juicy says, Damn, Pea. You gon let him diss you like that?

Bitch, was anybody talkin to you?

Who you callin a bitch? Juicy stops in her tracks and stands lookin through the fence, right at Shiheed.

Ain't but one bitch standin here. Maybe two.

Nigga, where yo mamma? I don't see that one-tooth bitch.

What, you gon talk bout—

Jus shut the fuck up, Juicy says. Yo breath stank.

Yo, Pea, Shiheed say. He lookin at me, big-ass nostrils aimed and cocked at my face, a sawed-off shotgun. I can't talk. I can't move. Yo. You better do sumpin bout yo ugly Hee Haw–lookin bitch.

Ugly? Nigga, how many mirrors ran away from you today?

Yo, Pea, you better put yo bitch on a leash.

Why don't you do it?

I'll wreck this bitch. You know I don't give a fuck. Straight jackin.

Juicy chuckles. Nigga, you can't even jack yo own dick.

Yo, Pea. I'm tellin you, been a long time since I put the screws to somebody.

Well, here's yo chance. Step to it. Be a man.

Nawl. Nawl. Bitch, you think I'm gon stomp you with yo kids right here in fronta you, watchin?

Crust and Ham lookin round fo weapons. Crust picks up a pop bottle and breaks it. Ham finds a piece a coat hanger. They assume war poses.

Bitch, you caught a break this time.

Anytime, Juicy says. You know where to find me. Then she turns to the kids, fulla venom. Yall put that down. Go ahead. They do what she tells them to do. Now, let's go. We wasted enough time wit this shit. He ain't nobody. They use to punk him in jail. We all start to walk off together.

Yo, Pea, Shiheed shouts. This shit all yo fault. Is you a man or is you a mouse? Nigga, you better learn how to smack the shit outta yo bitch every now and then.

Juicy chastises her kids. What I tell yall bout weapons?

But—

But nothing. I don't like repeatin myself.

The kids drop their heads, breathin all hard, ready to cry.

Yall better not start all that cryin. We can go on back to the house.

Okay, Mamma. We ain't gon cry.

We stop at the entrance to the El station. I can't look Juicy in the face.

Aw ight, she says. Don't forget my cigarettes.

I won't. I hurry off wit the kids.

The after-school hustle is set up to catch the rush-hour crowd. Of course, all the heads be out there too, in close proximity to the cash. Like, this Chinese nigga come walkin through the car, pullin along a lil cart behind him and screamin.

Ahhhhhhhhhhhhhhhhhhhhhh, battary battary, one dollahhhh-hhhhhhhhhhh! . . . Ahhhhhhhhhhhhhhhhhhhhhhhh, battary battary, one dollahhhhhhhhhhhhhhhhh!

You also got them old-school hustlers, like this one game-talkin nigga named Sinbad, who dress the part in this checkered sports shirt and these brown double-knit polyester slacks. Nigga pants is slack, all right—floods, all high above his white socks and black square-toed kicks. He kick that shit bout sumpin he call the Action Factor. He be like, A wise man once said, The gods weave misfortunes for men so that the generations to come will have something to sing about. But I say that we don't have to sing sorrow songs. You see, our boys are in the pit. We hand them the ladder to get out. We put them in school, train them, educate them, teach them that knowledge can give tongue to the winged cries of their souls. I know. I was one of those boys. But I stand before you now a new man. Help us light the torch of wisdom. Help us rekindle the fires of manhood. Help us chart the stars.

Won't you help us, the Action Factor. Won't you reach out your hand to us, Action Factor? Please help us, the Action Factor.

He come up to me, rattlin his can.

I jus look at him. Then I be like, I know you.

His eyes go scared. He hurry off.

When he leaves the car, I signal Crust and Ham. They pop up from they seats and move into the aisle.

Excuse me, ladies and gentlemen. Sorry to interrupt your conversation and readin pleasures. I'm Pork and I'm Chop, and together we the Pork Chop crew. We don't snatch chains, gangbang, or sling cocaine, or live in the correctional way. We jus tryin to earn a honest dollar. We gon tell you a lil story bout our grandma.

After Crust and Ham kick the introduction, I duck down inside that high-sided area right in fronta the doors, where nobody can see me, and I slip this old granny dress over my clothes and fit this old gray granny wig on my head.

A few grumpy-ass squares start complainin and shit. They be like, Hey, I don't wanna hear all that noise. Tell you what, I'll give you a quarter if you jus sit down and shut up. But the other riders squash all that drama. Who the fuck is you? If you don't want no noise, drive yo car to work. I paid my carfare, just like you, and I want some entertainment.

I start granny-walkin down the aisle, all bent over, like I got a cane.

> Got no food to eat and
> My feet got no beats
> My welfare check didn't come
> Not even a little sum
> They stole my radio

Hamfat and Crust, they be like, Why they do that, Granny?

> Guess they don't love they granny no mo.

People start crackin up, bent over in they seats, slob flyin off they tongues. I make it to the end of the aisle, balancin myself against the fast-movin train.

> It would be a big appreciation
> If you gave us a small donation.

We jus tryin to earn a honest dollar. If you don't jibe this time, maybe you'll jibe next time. Crust and Ham start comin down the aisle with their baseball caps stretched out to the people on both sidesa the train. I say, And we accept pennies, nickels, dimes, quarters, dollars, checks, transfers, tokens, and food stamps, and Crust and Ham say, And ladies' phone numbers. Everybody laugh. Good fo me. Laughter loosen up the wallets and purses. Once the kids reach me, we turn and face everybody. Thank you, ladies and gentlemen. I'm Pork. I'm Chop. And we the Pork Chop crew. Enjoy your evenin. We move on to the next car.

We start in the last car and work our way up to the front. Seven cars in all. Then we get off the train and catch one back in the opposite direction. We work it this way through rush hour. Not much money to make after that. And by then the kids start to bitch and whine bout how they tired and hungry and thirsty. So I let em share a candy bar until we make it down to Mickey D's so I can buy them a Yummy Deal.

I want my own King Mac.

He slobbered on the bun.

He put mustard on it.

Pickles is nasty.

He stole my fry.

Where the salt?

Ketchup is nasty.

He spit in the shake.

Hey, yall shut up, I say. Can't you see I'm tryin to think? I'm countin my ends in the dark space under the table, the boys positioned in fronta me, fo cover, on the other side. Shit. For the day, I pulled jus enough to maintain. I count it again. Shit.

I take Crust and Ham to the park to pump the swings for a while. I sit down on the hard splintery bench and watch them go up, down, up, down, their own lil competition. Who can swing the highest? When they get tired of the swings, they starts into feedin the pigeons, pitchin potato chips hard and fast, seein who can clobber the most birds. I'm thinkin the whole time. We leave the park jus as night starts to fall.

A block from the El station, Crust yells out, You ain't buy Juicy's cigarettes. Shit. So we swing into a corner sto. I'm hopin the owner won't card me, but he jus looks me up and down, takes my money, and places the squares on the counter. He even throws in an extra book of matches.

We head fo the station. I'm busy addin and subtractin as we walk. I got to pay full adult fare for me and reduced fare for the kids. By the time we make it to the station, I've come up wit this plan. I direct Crust and Ham right past the agent sittin in the glassed-in booth and right over to the large wall map. I'm standin there studyin all the routes and lines like I don't know where we goin.

I wait until I hear the train comin into the station. I says to the kids, Okay, remember what I told you. The train grinds to a stop, the doors pop open, and people come rushin out. Go on, I tell them. Duck under.

They duck under the turnstile. Then I duck under, but soon as I pop up, I see this transit dick standin in the do of the train, lookin at me. He say, What the deal, son? He reach to grab me, and I take off as fast as I can, hotfoot, the dick shoutin commandments behind me. Far as I can tell, Crust and Ham shoot off runnin in another direction. Either that, or they made it onto the train. I run in lil rushes of speed, curvin round iron beams, tryin to shake off the dick. I look back and see that I'm puttin some good distance between our bodies. That's when I feel my legs start to shut down, my steps get smaller, my ankles band together, like some cowboy done hooped me in a lasso. I trip and stumble face first toward the ground but break my fall in the nick of time wit my hands.

The dick come up behind me, breathin and coughin all hard. He reach down and jerk me to my feet. He keeps one hand on me, the other on his hip, and stands there swayin from side to side, tryin to catch his breath. Damn, he says, grinnin and shakin his head. They make you all dumber every day. Nobody never told you how to keep yo pants up?

What? I look down and see my jeans all tangled up around my ankles. I'm standin there in my draws. People is pointin and laughin.

You got enough room in there for an entire family.

Would you pull my pants up?

Maybe I should take your picture.

A second dick comes over with Crust and Ham. He takes one look at me and tells his partner, Pull his pants up. The first dick pulls up my pants. They start to walk away wit us.

JEFFERY RENARD ALLEN

Damn, he could run.

Couldn't he.

Need to put him in the Olympics.

Jesse Owens.

They take us back into this little office. That's when I get my firs good look at the two dicks. The dick who'd caught me ain't much older than myself. He got this lil lima-bean head and this peach fuzz on his chin, which he keep stuck way out for the world's admiration. The second dick older, a big ugly Frankenstein-lookin motherfucker. Round pigeon shoulders and muscular ears. Face all scrunched up and serious, like he bitin down on his words, snappin them in two. He shoves me into the wall. Okay, let's see some ID.

You lookin at it.

You don't have any ID?

I lost my wallet.

I'll go back and see if I can find it, Peach Fuzz says.

Nawl. I lost it a long time ago.

Monster Dick starts goin through my pants pockets, pullin the long insides out like banana peels. Look, I say, mind my civils.

Be quiet, Peach Fuzz says. Civil rights are for citizens. You're underaged.

What? Hey, I'm not—

Frankenstein shoves me into a chair. Sit there. Shut up. Then he bear-hugs the kids and starts pullin them toward his face like he gon screw them into his eyes. They start bawlin. Juicy! Juicy! Mamma! Mamma!

Hey, Officer, I say, don't scare the kids.

He lets them go and points to a chair. They squeeze into it. Then he stand there lookin at me. Mr. Hero, he says.

You shouldn scare the kids.

Mr. Hero.

I jus sit there watchin him, quiet.

Mr. Hero, let me ask you something.

I know my rights.

Come on, just one question. Off the record.

I watch him. Off the record?

I would have it no other way.

Aw ight, then.

Where will you be in five years?

Dead.

The dick's frown burns away.

But see, we criminals never die. I'll probably come back as a pimp or serial killer in my next lifetime. Maybe even the president.

His face seals over in anger. So, you one of those smart ones.

Look, I messed up. You caught me. Slippin. Can we get on with it? No disrespect. Can you jus gon and write my summons?

Wish we could, the young dick says, but we don't handle kids. City policy.

I ain't a kid.

He grins. Okay, if you say so. But what about them? He motions to Crust and Ham.

Can't we forget about them?

Wish we could. But I'm not getting caught up in a lawsuit.

Lawsuit?

Everybody wants to sue nowdays.

Look, I jus wanna—

I already told you. We don't handle kids. You don't like that policy, take it up with the city council. The mayor.

Man, I don't believe this.

The young dick sits down at his desk and starts fillin out some forms.

What? I got to wait fo you to do yo paperwork?

That's right. Then you'll go down to the Hundred-and-seventh Precinct.

I don't believe this.

Why don't you try to relax.

Frankenstein leanin against the wall beside the desk, lookin at me. I eye his badge: JASON GEORGE SAMS.

I be like, Hey, yall ain't even real cops. What kind of cop got three first names?

Frankenstein don't say a word.

Why don't you jus gon and call the *real* cops.

The transit dick puts his pen down and starts lookin at me. Hey, you want this to take all night? I didn't think so. Why don't you pipe down and relax. He starts back on his form.

Hey, Hero, Frankenstein says to me. You mind if I have one of your cigarettes?

What? You on the job.

Maybe I want to smoke it after I get off the job.

I'm thinkin, *Why this nigga fuckin wit me?* They ain't mine.

What, you stole them?

How you gon play me like that? Officer, I ain't no thief. I'm a sneak.

My mistake. So, Hero, let me just take one of your cigarettes, see, and I'll tell them to let you keep the pack. Otherwise.

Okay.

He removes Juicy's pack of squares from this plastic bag, opens it, and pulls outta square. He taps the butt, puts the square between his teeth, and fires it up wit his own lighter.

Hey, Jason, the other dick says, pass me one of those.

Jason holds out the pack fo the young dick, and he waste no time pullin outta square and firin it up. And the two of them jus start puffin like crazy, the young dick sittin there at his desk, strings of smoke risin up to the ceiling, jerkin him this way and that like he some kinda puppet. And the other one real relaxed against the wall, blowin fat white rings and cannonballs.

Hey, I say.

They look at me.

Ain't you heard?

Heard what?

Smokin is bad for you. Make yo balls shrink.

I guess that jus pissed em off big-time, cause they hurry up and finish those squares mad quick, then fire up two fresh ones. They smoke on those long and good, till they see these two city dicks approachin the office, strapped with gats, nightsticks, radios, handcuffs, and mace. The transit dicks stub out the squares in a glass ashtray and shove the ashtray into a metal drawer.

This him? one cop asks.

That's him.

Workin together, the municipal dicks pull me up from the chair and start pattin me down.

We already frisked him, Frankenstein says. Here are his effects.

They continue to frisk me. Satisfied, one dick takes the plastic bag from Frankenstein, the pack of squares inside. Paperwork?

Peach Fuzz holds out a form. The dick takes the form and folds it into his breast pocket. Two other city dicks come and take Crust and Ham into they custody. Jus befo the kids step outta the room, they turn to me and throw up they sign. I nod.

I guess we're about done here. Okay, son. Let's go.

We get on the elevator and rise up to the street like smoke up a chimney. Then they shove me in the back of this paddy wagon and slam the door shut. And I jus sit there like the last sardine in a can, dry and forgotten. Ain't gon lie, I'm scared as a motherfucker.

They hustle me into the precinct and we go in one room after another, the escortin dicks noddin to the station dicks. Seem like we walk damn near a mile. Finally, we come to this one tiny-ass room wit jus one dick, sittin at a desk, readin a sports magazine.

Hey, Steve, look who we got for you.

The dick named Steve looks up at me from his desk.

This here's—tell him your name.

I tell him my name.

Ain't he a beauty. I'm thinking I should take him home and make him my son.

Could I have him first? Steve tosses his magazine on top of a pile of papers on his desk.

Only if you say please.

Please.

Okay.

The cop shoves me into the chair next to Steve's desk and hands Steve the form and my personal effects. Steve takes a quick look at the form and flips it onto his desk.

Routine, he says.

That's right. Nothing special. Never is.

Thanks, guys.

The two dicks turn and head outta the room. Steve tapes the form to my personal-effects bag, then tosses the bag onto the desk. Halfway out the door, one of the departin dicks stops and turns back around. Hey, Steve?

Yeah.

You should show him our resident.

This one here?

Sure.

No, I don't think so.

Go ahead. It might do him some good. He leaves.

What resident? I ask.

Police matters. He sittin there writin sumpin on a clipboard.

How long is this gon take?

They'll release you from juvenile after you see a judge.

What? But I ain't underaged.

They'll have to verify all of that.

What? I'm thinkin, *They got all kindsa ways to fuck with you.* Officer, what's the charge?

Solicitation.

Solicitation? What? I ain't no pimp.

That's the charge.

Look, I'm jus tryin to make a livin.

It's still against the law.

Then somebody need to change the goddamn law.

The cop looks over at me. I'm sure they'll change the goddamn law for you. You're so wonderful. You're so essential to our long-term survival.

I snorted. Ain't this a bitch.

Could you do one thing for me? Steve says.

What?

Would you mind?

What?

Would you shut your fuckin mouth? Thank you.

So I jus sit there and shut the fuck up. What else I'm gon do?

There's something you don't realize, Steve says.

What's that, Officer?

I'm givin you a fuckin break here.

A break? Is that what you call it?

Yes, that's what we call it.

Okay. You the authority. I suck my teeth.

He lookin at me. You know what, we got theft of city services. Three counts. Endangerment of a child. Two counts. Corruption of a minor. Two counts. Fleeing the scene of a crime. One count. Evading arrest. One count. And one count of aggravated assault.

What's the assault for?

On the train platform you stepped on some lady's toe.

I jus slid down in my seat. These niggas is a trip.

You should be thanking me.

Thanks.

Okay, that's the paperwork. He flips the clipboard down on the desk. They'll be takin you over to juvy.

You already told me that.

So, I can't tell you again?

I ain't say shit, not one fuckin word.

Are we clear?

Yes, Officer.

Okay. So, they'll be taking you over to juvy. But before they do, I want to show you something.

What?

I'll show you.

Why?

Because you're such a smart and honest and delightful and handsome sonuvabitch.

You gon beat me or sumpin?

You think we really do that.

I jus look at him, and keep lookin.

Follow me.

So he gets up from the desk and I gets up from the chair, and I follow him through a door into a large room wit one cell, a good twelve feet high and wide and maybe ten deep. There's this one nigga inna cell, stretched out on this one cot, his hands behin his head and his feet crossed at the ankles.

Okay, Steve says. I'll leave you to it. He walks outta the room, shuts the door, and leaves me standin befo this stretched-out nigga.

The nigga looks over and sees me, and that's when I see his face for the firs time. Some old nigga. Well, maybe he ain't too old. His hair got nappy patches of gray, and gray hairs curl throughout his goatee. But the face is smooth. He swing his legs round and props to a sittin position, bent over, lookin down at his shoes. Then he be like, So, what they get you for? Talkin to his shoes.

Jumpin the turnstile.

They arrest people fo that now?

I chuckle. Nawl. They send you to college.

He looks up at me. Is that what they do? Sayin it like he don't know I'm dissin his ass.

So, Pops, what you doin back here?

What it look like I'm doin?

Not much. Jus sittin there. Hey, I really think I should bounce. Why don't I let you sleep it off.

You can't sleep off what I got.

I chuckle. Pops, they takin you to the rehab? Is that where you goin, the rehab?

Why would I need to go there?

You tell me.

Are you as dumb as you look? Any fool can see I'm here workin wit you.

Workin wit me? Okay, Pops. Really. Why don't I let you sleep if off. Hey, Steve.

Nigga, what's wrong? You afraid?

Afraid?

Don't stress yourself.

Afraid?

The cell locked.

Hey, Pops, I'm fin to bounce.

Nigga, you might as well relax. That door locked.

I look at the door, look at Pops, look at the door, look at Pops. Hey, what's this all about? You an officer? Aw ight, you got me. I'm scared.

Do I look like an officer?

I look him over. He wearin this kinda two-piece, a plain red shirt, no collar, and plain red sweats, and the material is all worn, with lint and loose thread. The shit look raw, like a plucked chicken. What they get you for?

You don't wanna know.

How long you been in?

Oh, about twenty-seben years.

What? Twenty-seven years?

Give or take.

I'm thinkin, Okay, he's one of the crazies. One of those loons who'll sneak up behin you and shove you off the platform. Maybe I do have me a lawsuit. Got me locked up in here wit some crazy. Cruel and unusual punishment.

I work fo the city. Around the clock. I help them with some of the problem cases.

Problem cases?

That's right.

I know he a crazy, but I don't let on. So that means I've graduated, I say.

Come again?

The dick out there called me a piece of shit. But now I graduated to a problem case.

Steve didn't say that.

Yes, he did.

He lookin at me. What's your name?

Didn't they tell you?

Would I be askin if they did?

Well, I don't feel like sayin.

Suit yoself. You know why they brought you back here?

You sure in the fuck are gonna tell me.

They want you to see my wings.

Thinkin, Oh man. I know I got me a lawsuit. You can fly?

Most winged creatures can.

I look around the room fo a chair or somewhere to sit. Shit.

I ain't stepped outta this cell since they arrest me. Twenty-seben years.

What bout when you haf to take a piss or a shit?

He jus look at me. You ain't sayin nothin but what's natural.

So, you a natural man too, huh, Pops?

No. I'm a public servant. And I'm damn good at it, and I enjoy my work. I got clean comfortable board. I get my rations and my commissary. And the pay ain't bad. Though I don't spend none of my salary. Ain't spend none in these twenty-seben years. I just have them put it all in the bank. I must be richer than Rockefeller by now. Maybe someday I'll leave it all to a young buck like you.

Fuck someday. I'll settle for a loan today.

No way. I can tell by the way you dressed you ain't got no collateral.

Pops, look at you. Don't talk bout the way nobody dressed.

Granted. We both men. He cough. Will you allow me to ask you a difficult question?

Why, Pops? What you got to ask me?

You drop outta school, didn you?

Nawl, Pops. I'm in college. I got to get my law degree so I can represent broke-ass motherfuckers like you.

Why you stop goin?

All they did was teach me how to curse.

You don't say? That's the same exact thing they taught me.

I get a real good laugh offa that one. Pops, you is funny. Real funny. You old niggas master them jokes. Man. So now I bet you gon tell me that you used to be like me?

I ain't never been like you. I ain't never been anything like you.

He just sittin there starin at me, eyes all glowin, and I'm thinkin, This motherfucker bout to go off. Better do somethin to calm his ass down. So, Pops, where yo wings?

You ready to see them? He starts to takin off his shirt, pullin his arms outta the sleeves.

Hey, hold up. I'm thinkin maybe I should go over and make sure the jail cell locked.

Don't worry, he says. I ain't no freak, he says.

Why don't you keep yo shit on. Jus tell me what you got to tell me.

But he pulls the shirt over his head and throws it onto the cot. He in pretty good shape fo an old man, the muscles in his arms and chest cut. He stands up. I'm hopin this nigga won't take off his pants.

Hey, Pops.

He spins his back slowly toward me, and, sure nough, he got wings. Lil wings, no bigger than yo hands, all folded up like paper planes or church fans.

Are those supposed to be real?

What you think?

I don't say anything.

Tell you what, why don't you touch them. Go ahead. Touch them.

Nawl, that's aw ight.

I step closer to the cell, a good five feet away from him, close enough to see but far enough away that I can jump back if I need to. The wings ain't got no feathers. They all dried up and brown and crusty, like some fried chicken wings.

You gettin a good look?

My tongue won't move.

You know what?

I can't speak.

These things cause me all sortsa trouble on the outside. Let me show you sumpin else. He moves, and I flinch and jump back. He starts climbin the bars up one sidea the cell like one of them circus acrobatics goin up a ladder, and then, when he gets to the toppa the cell, he eases around wit his hands on the bars behin him and stretches his body forward, out over the bed, ten feet below, lockin his arms, stiff triangles behin him. Then he lets go of the bars.

He falls straight forward and stops in midair, body horizontal, that cot a good five feet beneath him. Holy shit. What did I jus see? Those lil wings are movin up and down, up and down. Like a skydiver, he rises straight up to the toppa the cell, then he starts slidin forward on the air, all the way to the end of the cell, then he turns and comes back the other way, and he goes on this way fo quite some time, flyin about the cell, makin sharp turns cause it ain't much room to maneuver, flyin like this a good ten minutes befo he swoops down and sits himself on the cot.

I'm standin there lookin. His fohead and chest and neck are bright wit sweat. He takes a good look at me. Then he be like, I don't need to tell you what you jus saw.

I wish I could speak.

Don't worry, son. One big jump, the real men get there.

If I could jus speak.

Well, he says, I guess that bout does it, wouldn you say?

I nod, my neck stiff.

Good. Hey, befo you leave, do me a favor, would you?

What? My voice is quiet, a scratch.

Get the keys from Steve.

I'm lookin at him.

Jus jokin.

Just then, the do swings open and Steve pops in. All done here?

All done. You got a towel?

Sure. Steve tosses Pops a towel and motions fo me to follow him into the other room. I do. In fact, I follow him all through the entire station, back to the precinct entry. Then he turns and looks at me. You ain't got to say a word. You free to go. The city allows you a token. He drops the transit token into my hand.

I ask no questions and step out to the street. And I wanna think bout my personal effects and Juicy's squares, wanna think bout this flyin nigga I jus seen and bout all the other trippy shit that happen to me today. I wanna think bout all that, but the minute my foot hits the pavement, it starts to rain, hard and fast, rainin punches. Shit. Now don't this beat all? I put my head down and run faster than the rain to the El station. I stand near the turnstile and check to see how dry I am. Can say I'm wet but can't say I'm soaked.

I open my hand and, you guessed it, the token gone. What the fuck else can happen? I jus stand there a minute, searchin through my pockets, and, the next thing I know, I feel myself liftin into the loosenin air, my feet three inches above the ground. And I don't rise no higher than jus those three inches. I've levitated on the regular every day since. Always three inches. No lower, no higher.

Shimmy

I know I am not alone.
– JUNE JORDAN

Lee Christmas entered the street on a Sunday afternoon telling himself, Something fine is going to happen to me today. He had no sooner thought this, when he stepped into the full glare of the sun. As protection against the sticky yellow light and heat—were his underarms sweating? Stink follows sweat—he considered going back inside his house for an umbrella. Decided against it. The car would provide sufficient shield. The zoo would be shady. Here was the plan (words spoken in the darkness) as he and Peanut, his new lady, his main squeeze, had arranged it while returning—his hands cool and easy on the steering wheel—from their date the previous night. Lee would get to meet Boo, Peanut's seven-year-old son. The three of them would spend the afternoon at the zoo. Lee could imagine her hanging on tight to his arm and the kid tagging along beside them. After the zoo, they would show Boo Lee's office. Next, they would go out for dinner. Finally, they would go back to Lee's place. The adults would put Boo to bed so they themselves could *talk*. Though neither had said it, Lee took this to mean that their relationship had remained virgin long enough. He would rise refreshed after a vigorous night of love. Drive Boo to school. Peanut to the Look It Over Lounge, where she worked as a barmaid.

His white BMW gave back the sun's glitter. He got inside and found it full of sun. Though two years from forty, he dressed in the latest fashions, like a man half his age. White linen blazer and matching slacks. Red silk collarless shirt. Tan cowhide belt. White silk socks. Black espadrilles. After the date, he'd gotten a house cut. Hair prickly at the sides and in the back. As thick and square as a privet hedge on top. Nineteen years Peanut's senior. Felt the need to look young for her.

The engine roared to life. His custom, he drove the white BMW with hands gripping the steering wheel, palms spreading cupfuls of sweat. At times he believed that the sun was actually drumming on the roof of the car. He turned down his blinds. Sunlight shimmered on the windshield. Fell squarely against his face. The car reached Turtle Avenue. X-rated marquees swam into focus. *Love, Gestapo-Style. Studboy. DD Movie. The Plumber of Love. He's the plumber of love, wrecking homes with a foot of pipe.* Electricity ran the rails of Lee's legs, to his groin.

Peanut and Boo lived in this neighborhood. She claimed they leased a small studio apartment. Lee had never seen it.

I can't let you come in, cause it sort of junky and whatnot.

I'm not afraid of a little junk, Lee said.

Yeah, but I am.

Lee would always park in front of her building and honk his horn. Then she would come downstairs.

Peanut had told him that she sometimes left Boo home by himself. He can take care of himself and whatnot.

But he's just seven.

He smart. He like a lil ole man.

But he's just seven.

Peanut flashed him a cold look. Look, mind yo own business.

I'm just trying to—

Well, I don't need yo advice. I don't tell you what to do.

I could get you a babysitter.

Just mind yo own business.

I'm sorry. Lee hated being forced to apologize. He could live with it.

Peanut still hadn't said anything.

After some time she said, Apology accepted. Just don't do it again.

I won't.

Yes, this was Peanut's neighborhood. It was bad. Not real bad, but bad enough. Would he visit her if she lived in the projects? Probably. She was the right woman for him. He looked at his watch. Solid gold, with diamond strips for the markings. He still had thirty minutes. Peanut would have something nasty to say if he arrived early. He circled back, found a shady spot on a side street near an X-rated theater, and parked the car. Quiet slipped through the shut windows, along with traces of sun and heat.

Boo happened after an indiscretion and whatnot, Peanut had said.

An indiscretion? Lee asked.

Yeah. An indiscretion. I had Boo when I was twelve.

Twelve?

Yeah. Twelve. I wasn't as smart then as I am now.

Wow. Twelve.

But he's my baby, and I love him mo than anything in this world, even if his father *is* a stupid bastard and whatnot.

Lee hadn't pursued it. He understood the maternal instinct. A bond greater than any *indiscretion*. Peanut was in love with him. Even if she wasn't, she was the right woman for him.

They had met two weeks ago at the Look It Over Lounge. Lee's daughter, Samantha, had run away from home, and he had decided to celebrate. The bar drew him like a magnet. He put on an Italian double-breasted suit. Three-hundred-dollar alligator shoes. Slipped on his two best diamond rings. Drove to the lounge. Lee rarely drank, and then, only a mild cocktail. Peanut fixed him a piña colada. The liquor's warmth relaxed him. He detected a flicker of interest in Peanut's face. Didn't let the opportunity slip by. He stuck around. Made small talk. Quitting time, Peanut invited him to her hangout, the Southway Lounge. The heat of a second piña colada unfroze his tongue. He explained that he owned the Black Widow Exterminating Company. Had accounts with many of the best office buildings in this city and neighboring cities. Revealed that he owned six buildings, valued at a million dollars each.

How old are you? She squeezed one of his biceps. He had done his push-ups and pumped some iron at home. He needed to do something about his belly. Had seen an X-rated movie where a woman made her partner keep his shirt on while they had sex. She couldn't stand the sight of his potbelly. Lee had decided to work out daily. Burn off the fat.

Old enough, baby girl. He decided not to reveal his age. Peanut smiled, leaving him to believe she enjoyed the mystery about his age. Lee had inherited his father's height but not his good looks. Everyone always thought he was older than he was.

They stepped out onto the dance floor. Lee's back was board stiff. His hips failed to twist. Peanut was as good as he was clumsy. Shook the devils in her hips. Lee decided to take dancing lessons.

They'd gone to the Southway Lounge every night since. Lee had applied himself, with an ever-increasing determination, to impressing Peanut. Flowers. Dinners. Cards. *Exercise.*

He'd also decided not to reveal anything about the only woman in his past. While giving birth to Samantha, his wife had died, on the second anniversary of his company. He hadn't related his sixteen miserable years with Samantha. She was a fat, black, ugly, stanky, bald monster, mouth frozen in a permanent sneer—rubbery lips forever smeared with chicken grease or marzipan—a cold glitter in her eyes. She couldn't move without dragging her food-heavy feet. God, why did I name her after my mother? he thought. He couldn't think of another name, and his wife's name, Loretta, was pain and loss. It was spite for him that got Samantha a cashier's job at Hi-Lo Foods. Spite that made her give customers items for free. Fired after two weeks. You'd think a girl who did well in school would have better sense. Couldn't do anything right, couldn't cook or sew or wash dishes or mop a floor or wash a load of clothes without messing up. And always feeling sorry for herself. (Once he peeped through her bedroom keyhole and saw her doing a slow drag all by herself, her fat body a toy top wobbling out its last revolutions.) Yes, and the night she ran away from home, the night he found out that she was fucking the most notorious thug in the neighborhood, CC ... Yes, CC, who liked to string up cats and set fire to them. Liked to snatch ladies' purses and knock old folks upside the head.

That night Lee had a strange dream. He was a bird flying over a body of water. The sun hot and his wings heavy with sweat. He couldn't see his own body, but the shadow of his outstretched wings moved over the water. The sky darkened. His moving shadow turned white. The water changed to blood. Lee got tangled in the new tree-thick darkness. Moved his sweaty wings. Managed to break free. He changed into a bird of fire that singed the sky and left it black.

When he awoke, his mouth was dry, his neck stiff—both stuffed with cotton. A glass of water beckoned him into the kitchen. CC rushed into his vision. CC, in Lee's kitchen, all toothpick arms and potbelly. Sam butt naked beside him, holding his elbow. Beyond belief. How could the human body contain such fat? In one motion, CC grinned and zipped up his pants. Lee grabbed the nearest thing he could find, a jar of strawberry jelly. Hurled it at CC's head. A red fire-quick blur spurted out the door, laughing all the while. The jar shattered against the door, leaving a red blob like in one of those fancy paintings in the ritzy office buildings.

Got to throw better than that, old motherfucker, CC said from outside the door.

Lee kept the words at arm's distance. Spoke. Are you fucking that bastard?

Daddy, talk to me with some love. Samantha ran out—the fastest Lee had ever seen her move—after CC. Lee had not seen her since.

The night he met Peanut, he heard someone messing with the locks on the kitchen door. Samantha and CC. The following morning he had all the locks changed—though the locksmith had found no evidence of tampering—and bars put on all the windows.

That part of his past, Lee had to keep locked away. And there was more. He hadn't told Peanut that his mother had killed his father and then herself.

That he had spent the first eighteen years of his life in Keepback, Mississippi, a small, isolated, all-black community. The nearest town more than twenty miles away. The civil rights movement a continual event sparkling in the glass-eyed television. Lynching and Klan atrocities echoed like folktales given a horrible twist. White people: gray blots on television. Cataracts. And when the old folks spoke of these blots, Lee wondered if whites were foreigners from another country or even beings from another world.

Lee, his mother, and his father lived in a small house before a field of pear trees. During slavery, Keepback had been a single plantation. Their house was the only structure that remained from those days. The old folks said it had been the main nigger's quarters. Lee's father had transformed it into a library with books on science, math, and business. During the day, Lee went to school. At night his father taught him to manage receipts and figure accounts. Then he studied books from the library until he retired to bed.

The townspeople were farmers. They grew squash, tomatoes, and sorghum, for molasses, and black-eyed peas, corn, collard greens, watermelons, and cantaloupes. Though the house where Lee lived was modest, it was a mansion in comparison with the farmers' shacks. Keepback had poor irrigation; a good harvest was rare. They lived in wooden shacks with wooden floors. They pumped their water from wells. They shat in outhouses, a phone directory–thick Sears Roebuck catalog near at hand. Lee's family enjoyed furniture, carpeting, and comfortable beds. A bathroom. Indoor plumbing that Pop had installed. Pop had converted the front part of the house into a grocery and liquor store. Pop owned one of the few automobiles in town, a blue pickup truck. Bought liquor from Canton, fifty miles away. Brought it back to his store and sold it at twice the price paid. Gave out free beer once a month. Kept a fishbowl of free gumdrops for kids. Kept all his money in a safe behind his counter.

Pop had fought in the Second World War. The only black soldier to receive seven Silver Stars. After the war, he made one fabled city in the north his new port of call. Fell from a commuter platform. Lost a leg to a train. Screwed in a wooden one in its place. Took a train back home. In Canton, purchased the ex-slave's quarters— from a white real-estate agent—with his army savings. Lee recalled his father—the smooth pebble of his face carried forever in Lee's pocket—nearly seven feet tall and weighing well over three hundred pounds, stomping about without a cane or crutches. One size-fifteen foot and one peg leg. Hands made for a man half his size. Dark skin as smooth as a baby's behind. The leg and his teeth— each tooth like a rail tie across the length of Lee's memory—were his only ugly features.

Lee's mother was small and frail. Had been consumptive at her birth. Pop liked to say she was uglier than death. Mamma would blush. He'd add, Maybe God don't like ugly, but I do. She spent most of her time stooped over the vegetable and flower garden in the backyard. Kept a horseshoe over every door in the house. Religious. Serious with the gravity of one who read the Bible and attended church. Took Lee to the Mount Zion Baptist Church every Sunday. After her house, the church was the most impressive structure in the town. A brass cross mounted on its facade. Carpeted floors and overhead fans.

Pop never attended church, pissed off because no one in town drank on the Sabbath. In protest, he got drunk every Sunday in the town square—where four streets fanned from where he stood—and in full view of the church. Sunday nights, Mamma would chastise Pop about his un-Christian behavior.

Lee was seven:

Gypping people out they money with yo high liquor prices. Getting drunk in front of the church.

So what?

You wrong.

Wrong?

You jus wrong.

I gives them what they want.

You stealin.

So?

You blasphemous.

So?

That ain't Christian.

I don't hear Christ complaining.

You blasphemous.

Who ain't?

Heathen.

I won't be called names in my own house.

It started.

Pop punched Mamma. She fought back. He busted her lip. She uppercut his chin. He punched her eye. She snatched his wooden leg out from under him, pushed him to the floor, and knocked him upside the head with the leg.

After Mamma had knocked Pop out, she and Lee dragged him off to bed. They sat down in the kitchen together.

Mamma started singing.

Speak, Lord.
Speak to me.

Water drained from Lee's eyes.

Cry, baby, cry, Mamma said. She touched a ball of cotton to her lip. Wipe yo weepin eyes.

She touched the cotton to her lip.

Cry, baby, cry. Wipe yo weepin eyes.

I ain't no crybaby, Lee said.

Then why you cryin?

Pop hit you.

So? Do you see me cryin?

Nawl. But he hit you.

But I ain't cryin.

Why not?

Ain't got nothin to cry bout.

But he hit you.

How come you gon cry, if I ain't gon cry?

He hit you.

We make a deal. I won't cry, if you won't.

Lee is ten:

In the library, he studied his father. Avoided the man's eyes. This way he hoped to close out his mother's suffering. Block out the deep hurt that showed in his father's face. Pop put one small hand over the stump where it fitted into the hinge of his wooden leg. He deserved to suffer. Lee wished that he could make the pain worse.

Silent, his father retired to bed.

Lee stole away to his mother. Rubbed wintergreen alcohol on her wounds. Massaged cocoa butter into her scars. He invented his own space, his own world. Mamma's lumpy flesh a bag full of stones beneath his hands. The wintergreen a weak wind tickling his nose.

I should just take you and go away.

That's right, Mamma.

He ain't no good for you.

No good.

But he need me.

No, he don't. The wintergreen made Lee sneeze. He concentrated harder on his world.

I need him.

No, you don't.

He needs us.

Let's go.

Where we going? He need me. I love him.

Lee was eighteen:

New muscle. He worked up the courage to confront Pop.

Pop.

What?

Don't hit my mamma.

What? He gave Lee a cold glance. Lee had expected a blow.

Well, suh—he felt his courage slipping—she might kill you.

Pop looked at him. Did she tell you that? He showed his teeth.

No, suh. It's just that people don't like nobody hitting on them.

Pop's lips strained over the stalactite of teeth, biting in a laugh. Lee?

Yes, suh.

Pop leaned in close. A fever reached Lee's face. That's the best way a man can die. At the hands of the woman he loves.

Yes, suh. Lee didn't know what else to say. Some feeling struck him at the root of his belly.

Lee?

Yes, suh.

What is an avenue?

What did his question have to do with anything?

What is an avenue?

I never heard of that, suh.

I'll tell you. It's a type of street made like a U. You go down one way, and when you get to the end, it curves back around like that. He demonstrated with his small hands. It's like that horseshoe up there. He pointed to the object over the door.

Yes, suh.

They got many avenues in Paris. Saw them during the war. They make their streets real close to a curb. This close. He used his hands. We'd drive by in a jeep and some joker be standing on the street and we drive by and slap him just like that, slap that joker right upside the head. Only time in my life that I got to hit white folks. He laughed.

Lee laughed. He saw nothing funny.

Up north, they like to call everything an avenue. When you go up there, don't be fooled.

Yes, suh. When? Lee thought. He had no plans.

If it don't look like that horseshoe, it ain't an avenue.

Yes, suh.

That night, Lee's mother stood in the kitchen, hard at work with her foldout closet board. Her new electric iron. The only woman in town who could afford one. She sprinkled water from an empty pop bottle onto Pop's shirt. She was singing.

> *Will the circle be unbroken?*
> *Yes, Lord, bye and bye. Oh*
> *Yes, Lord, bye and bye.*

Mamma?

Baby.

He might kill you. He mean to.

No. I'm gon kill that nigger.

When?

Lord, forgive me.

When?

You know it wrong to kill.

But he gon kill you.

Let me tell you something.

What?

A person kills with the head and not the heart.

These were just words for Lee.

He tell you all that stuff bout a man needin brains and discipline. Well, I say this. Give your brains to books, but give your heart to Jesus.

Lee couldn't confess that since the age of about seven—yes, he'd concealed the secret that long—he hadn't believed in God. He didn't believe in the goings-on at the Mount Zion Baptist Church. Don't let him kill you.

He can't kill me. The Lord take me when it's my time to go.

The following Sunday, he and Mamma walked out of the church, into the blazing shimmering sun, and there was Pop, in the square, his wooden leg blazing fire. Pop had dropped his bottle. Or it had spilled from his fingers. He had doused himself in alcohol. The hot sun had ignited it. A hot wind whipped Lee's pants legs. The heat beat into his back and legs. Mamma took off after Pop. Lee shielded his eyes from the sun, which sprayed like buckshot in his face. Maybe the fire would burn Pop's entire body.

Mamma tackled Pop. He fell backward, slipping on an invisible banana peel. Mamma smothered the flames with her short torso, no longer than Pop's leg. From where he lay, Pop punched Mamma in the face. The blow threw her off the smoking leg—maybe fingers of flame had pushed her hot—onto the square's pavement. Lee walked home, alone.

That night, Lee changed the cotton gauze he had placed over the gash above Mamma's eye. Withdrawn so far into his own space, even the smell of wintergreen couldn't reach him.

Lee?

Ma'am?

You a man.

Yes, ma'am.

Do something for me.

Ma'am?

Remember. Give your heart to Jesus.

He tried to kill you.

Yes. And a person can be a fool for only so long. Her voice exploded in Lee's mind. He concentrated on his space.

The following morning, Lee discovered Mamma had buried a hatchet in Pop's head. The red blade indistinguishable from the red of the head. Mamma had slit her throat with a knife, the butcher knife that had cut bread gripped firm in her hand, to prevent it from slipping away. Blood swam in Lee's head and red-hot fish swam in the blood.

Lee put the bodies in two liquor crates. Buried them in the yard behind the house. Took the money from the safe. Slipped inside the blue truck. Drove north.

The city didn't surprise Lee. But the light was different. Every day he could taste the sun on his tongue like salt.

To save his money, he got himself a small studio apartment, drank water, and ate peanuts and liver sausage. Managed the Red Rooster, a greasy chicken joint, while attending business school at night. Concentrated on accounting and systems analysis. Finished school. Found employment with BAM, Black Accountants on the Move, and, when the opportunity came, bought the Black Widow Exterminating Company. Thought sharp. Dressed sharp. Slapped on the best cologne. Knew he could impress no one with his face. Then he met Loretta.

She was nineteen.

Stood, dark, behind the cashier's counter at the Lucky Seven, a small grocery store. (As he would learn, she lived in a small room above the store. Slept on a bed with a thin mattress. Stacks of spirit-filled books crowded the room from floor to ceiling.) Yes, dark. Almost black. Had she survived a fire? Her hair short. Her body thin. Even thinner in baggy men's chinos. She had large black eyes that made you want to look into them.

As a first step in resurrecting his new company, Lee developed new products that could be sold to the average customer. His chemists had started a new product, Rat Hotel—it would soon spark the public's interest and put the company back on its feet—and Lee was personally bringing it to stores and asking store owners to give free samples to customers.

Is the owner in?

No.

Lee explained his product and purpose.

Why do you want to kill rats? Loretta asked.

It's what I do for a living. Lee laughed. A genuine laugh for a genuine joke.

Don't you know that every rat has a soul?

He could tell that she was serious. Large black eyes, two little pools of oil. He caught himself. He was slipping in. That's one I never heard before.

Everything has a soul. Don't you know about reincarnation?

No.

Why not?

I don't believe in God.

Why not?

I've never seen him. He chuckled, hoping to lighten things up.

Don't waste your time looking for a Christian God. He don't exist.

Well, what kind of god are you talking about? Are you a Buddhist?

I ain't no Buddhist. But I know a little bout that too. We live in a multidimensional universe. God is all the dimensions.

Lee had to consider this.

Here, I got a book for you. Her hand disappeared under the counter. Emerged gripping a worn paperback. Slid it toward him.

He read the entire thing that night. Found it totally unconvincing, but it gave them something to discuss the following day. She gave him another book. He read it. The pattern was set. Their conversations continued. Reincarnation. Soul mates. Astral traveling. Demon possession. The eternal validity of the soul. Ghosts. He felt warm whenever she was near. When she spoke about a subject, her deep black eyes held a small but intense light. Lee warmed by the glow of her body beneath the baggy men's clothes. The feeling was strange and good. But there was also a feeling of desperation and separation. He was glad that she led the conversation; however, about her past, she formed an impenetrable wall. All he knew: she'd had a difficult childhood. Or so he figured. She never discussed her family. One day they came close to destroying the barrier:

My mamma, she say that death is in our pocket all the time, Loretta said.

What else does she say?

Not too much.

Is your mother alive?

Maybe.

Is your father alive?

Maybe.

How come you won't tell me? Don't you trust me?

No.

Why not?

I don't know. She sounded sincere.

My parents are dead.

Don't tell me.

My mamma—

She put her hands over her ears. Don't tell me.

And he never did.

It was more than three months after they met before they made love. The romance started with Lee giving her chaste kisses on the cheek. And she loved to hug. Started wearing dresses and tight-fitting pants. Tried to grow her hair long.

One night, in her book-crowded room above the store, she clutched him tightly. He was amazed at her strength. Was she trying to squeeze his spirit into her body? She smelled like a woman. Especially when he buried his nose in her short hair. He didn't know how long they'd been hugging, but after what must have been at least a half hour, her hug hadn't weakened.

I'll always be here for you, Lee said.

All men say that.

Well, I just ain't all men. He laughed. I love you.

I don't need your love.

Everybody needs love. He hated saying this. Loved her but hated saying it.

You just want a hole to stick your dick in.

Lee felt a tug in his chest. Loretta had never used such language before. No. I love you, he said.

Well, keep your love. Tender feelings are pointless.

He kissed her forehead.

Keep your kisses.

He kissed her cheek.

I don't need your kisses.

He kissed her neck. He continued. His kisses soft and slow, and searching. Following the soft curves of her body until they found her lips.

The first time Lee and Loretta made love, she wouldn't let him get on top. She got on top of him and moaned down in his face. He kept his eyes open. He didn't want to miss anything. Afterward, their bodies were covered with sweat as light as dew. He could taste the salt.

A month later, they married. Without ceremony. They got three witnesses—three of Lee's employees—and said their vows before the justice of the peace. So Loretta wanted it. Not that Lee had a single friend.

Life flowed fine during the first months of their marriage. The business was coming along. Lee purchased his first buildings. They leased a large apartment. Loretta quit her job at the grocery store. Lee ran the business during the day, while Loretta explored her interest in the paranormal. One day, Lee arrived home from work and saw Loretta in the kitchen with a glass of tea.

Lee?

What?

I need your help.

Anything for you, baby girl.

Help me find somebody.

A strange request. She had never mentioned any friends.

Who?

Phil.

Lee's skin got hot. Who?

Phil. He dead.

Lee laughed until his stomach hurt.

He dead. Loretta sipped her tea. Her eyes black stones in her face.

Dead?

Got killed in a car accident.

Lee didn't say anything.

On Easter. Four years ago. I need to find him.

Now I heard everything, Lee thought. He decided to play along.

We was in love.

Something kicked inside Lee's belly.

But he was married and had a child.

So you want me to resurrect your dead lover? Lee avoided her black eyes. He could taste the bitterness in his voice.

Don't be jealous.

I'm not jealous.

I love you.

Oh, I see. But you love him too?

That was a long time ago.

Not long enough.

Don't be that way. I love you.

Right.

I just need to find him and find out if he all right.

He dead, ain't he?

I love you. Don't be jealous. I need to know if he all right.

Jesus.

Sometimes when a person dies so badly, their soul can't rest.

Which book is that from?

He ain't no danger to you. I was fifteen. He was twenty-five. A grown man.

Lee didn't say anything.

It was a long time ago. He was married and had a child.

Did you fuck him too?

Now, don't be like that. We never did anything but kiss. A couplea times we grinded. But he was married and had a child.

Lee actually felt a little better.

It was a long time ago.

Okay. What do you want me to do? He would play along. Stupid to be jealous of a dead man. What harm could it do? She'd see that all this talk about the soul was just that, talk.

We need a Ouija board.

The next day Lee bought a Ouija board. For months they held hands and tried to make the pointer move. Nothing happened. They attended séances and consulted mediums. Nothing happened. Loretta would lock herself in a closet and read for hours.

One night they spread molasses on the Ouija board. Loretta had read that sweet sticky food helped to attract spirits. Lee had to fight to keep from laughing. They held hands before the board. Nothing happened.

That night, Loretta lay curled in his arms, as always. Her teeth were clicking. A sound like abacus beads knocked together.

The following morning her black skin glowed.

I saw Phil last night.

What?

He came to me in a dream.

Oh.

He said something to me, but I couldn't understand it. His voice was all muffled.

Didn't God, the Overlord of all the dimensions, teach him how to talk? She had gone just too far.

She looked at him. I don't need your sarcasm.

Who's being sarcastic?

His voice sounded like a growl, she said. Like it had to come up from his belly.

What are you telling me, that God put the man's mouth in his belly?

It had a lot of pain.

Lee didn't say anything.

That night, Loretta's teeth made the same sounds. In the morning her skin was radiant.

Lee, Phil's going to teach me how to talk to spirits.

Wonderful.

Now, don't be that way.

What? Carry on your dialogue with the dead.

Now—

He can't talk himself. How is he going to teach you to talk with the dead?

She just looked at him.

How can you understand what he says?

Don't ask stupid questions.

I'm not asking stupid questions.

You're just jealous.

Fire moved over Lee's skin. Why should I be?

Don't play games.

You're the one who's playing games. He left for work.

He returned that evening to an apartment smelling of gasoline and burned rubber. The smell led him to the bedroom. He heard Loretta moaning. Lee opened the door. He saw Loretta with her legs spread and a man between them. A strange-looking black man. With long red hair that hung to his shoulders. Standing up, he was probably as tall as Lee. But skinny. So skinny that his bones showed beneath his yellow skin. His back glistened with sweat.

Get your dead ass off my wife, Lee said.

Phil—who else could it have been?—stopped pumping Loretta. Turned his head and looked Lee in the face. He was beautiful. You aren't speaking to just anybody, you know, he said, in a voice so deep that it might have come out of a cannon. A tear brightened his eye. He evaporated, steam on a mirror.

Lee saw Loretta's black eyes. She pulled the bedsheet over her face. Lee fled the house. Found a room in a motel, and there he remained.

Only in that room did it dawn on Lee that he had seen a ghost. He didn't fear it. The ghost's existence contradicted the world as he knew it. But this wasn't the important thing. He had other fears, and he had anger too. He didn't understand what the ghost saw in Loretta. He was beautiful. She was ugly. That's all there was to it. And he loved her enough to return from the dead. And Lee loved her too.

A week later, he returned home. Loretta was sitting in the kitchen with a glass of tea. Lee looked at her shadow, quivering on the wall.

I swear on my mother's grave that I love you. How could you do this to me?

Loretta poked at a lemon slice. I had to know if he was all right. What?

I felt so bad. I had to know if he was all right.

Lee felt her reaching out for him. What do you mean? He lifted his eyes to meet hers.

I just felt so bad inside.

Loneliness washed over Lee, burning his body. He took what she said with a glad heart, even if she didn't love him. Without her, life would run out of him.

I just felt so bad.

Lee didn't say anything. Her words were concrete. He could weigh them in his hands.

Come here.

This he did.

About a month later, Loretta discovered that she was pregnant. She began to want ice cream for every meal. A month later, she bought a ten-pound bag of candy. Lee attributed this strange diet to maternal craving. The next month, she purchased a bag of balloons, filled them, and taped them everywhere in the apartment. Next, she filled their bedroom with stuffed animals. Once, Lee tried to kiss her, and she moved away, giggling. And when he tried to stroke her breasts, she replied, Unh. That's nasty. You mannish. Each month brought a new element. In the ninth month, Lee caught her jumping rope with her full belly. As it was, on her skinny frame her belly was so large that Lee wondered why she never fell forward. And here she was, skipping rope. Lee spent more than an hour chasing her through the apartment. Catch me if you can, she said. He cornered her. Eased her into a chair.

The day she entered the hospital to deliver their child, she entered a world he didn't belong to.

Lee moved to another city. The business and the buildings—he bought more—were really making money now. Money in his hand—as common as day and night. He bought a house. Hired a servant to care for Samantha (raised by one servant or another until she was thirteen—each year bringing a new slab of fat and a new servant to tend it—when Lee felt she was old enough to care for herself). Loretta's death left a hole inside Lee that he didn't know how to fill. He read her books, attended séances, consulted mediums, worked the molasses-sticky Ouija board. Loretta never returned to him. Never visited him in dreams. He had to suffer alone with a fat ugly daughter who never asked about her mother. It was only when Samantha ran away from home that he decided to cut loose from the past. He still loved Loretta. But maybe he could grow to love Peanut too.

And there he was, on a shady side street right off Turtle Avenue. This isn't a real avenue, Lee thought. Days before, driving Peanut home from the Southway Lounge, he had tried to explain this to her.

You know, this isn't a real avenue. Lee had had both hands on the steering wheel.

What you mean?

Like I said. It's not a real avenue.

Can't you spell? The signs say it. Turtle Avenue. A-v-e—

I know. But it's still not a real avenue. A real avenue is made like a horseshoe.

What are you talkin about?

I'm tryin to explain.

God. Sometimes you talk about the most boringness stuff.

It isn't boring. Lee didn't mean to let his anger slip out.

Oh yeah?

Why don't you let me explain?

I don't want to hear about no avenue.

Okay. The hot feeling still moved over his skin.

Another night on the avenue, they discussed Boo's father.

His father always be tryin to come by and see Boo and whatnot.

Why don't you let him?

Lee could feel her eyes on him. Boy, you is really dense.

Lee laughed.

I told you. I don't believe in messin wit no butt hole.

Lee didn't know if she was calling him that or Boo's father. I see.

He buy Boo clothes and toys and whatnot. Give me money. Bring some food by sometimes.

Well . . . Lee watched his words, careful not to say the wrong thing. That's good.

Yeah, but that's all I let him do. I make Boo go in the bathroom when that butt hole come by.

I see.

A week ago, Lee had first learned of Boo. He had taken Peanut to his office. He leased the fiftieth floor of the Garden Tower, one of the most distinguished office buildings in the city. The Black Widow Exterminating Company at one end of the hall, and Archer Realty, his other company, at the opposite end. His office was the size of a four-room apartment. A glass-and-steel box that projected out from the side of the building. Floor-to-ceiling windows. Marble floors. His desk centered on a single rug. As long as a dining table. With an ivory inkstand with a pen, and a telephone on its top. (Lee never used the phone or the pen. Rarely came to the office. A group of lawyers and executives ran the company. For years, Lee had spent most of his time searching for Loretta.)

Wow, Peanut said. Her voice echoed.

You like it?

This place bigger than my apartment.

Stupid, Lee thought. Of course it was bigger than her apartment. She lived in a studio. Yes, he said.

What kind of rug is that? She moved forward to get a closer look. Her footsteps drum taps on the marble.

It's from Afghanistan.

You been there?

No. Lee had no interest in traveling. It's completely handwoven. Every thread.

God. It musta took somebody a long time to finish.

Another stupid thing to say. Lee played along with it. I guess so.

Boo would like this place. She looked around.

Boo?

My son.

Oh.

His real name is Goodwin Junior.

Lee nodded.

After his father and whatnot.

How old is he?

He seven.

I didn't know that you had a son.

Now you do.

Lee didn't like being insulted in his own office.

Why do you call him Boo?

Cause he scare me.

He scares you?

Yeah. His love be so strong.

I don't follow.

Boy, is you dense.

Lee didn't say anything.

I can't deal wit no dense folks.

I just don't understand what you mean.

She rolled her eyes. Look, Boo love so strong for me that it scare me.

Oh. I see.

Finally.

Lee didn't say anything.

Anyway. Don't you want to meet him?

Only if he don't scare me.

Peanut just looked at him. That joke sure was corny and whatnot.

Lee felt delighted. His heart glowed inside. She'd missed his sarcasm.

Boo won't scare you.

Good.

I want him to see yo office.

Sure. When are we going to bring him by? Next Sunday? That was Peanut's day off.

Bet. A week from today.

Okay. Sunday, then.

Bet.

Lee was tugged by two feelings. On the one hand, he didn't like kids. On the other, Boo's existence offered him the chance to start a real family. Boo wasn't his own child, but Lee was certain that he could learn to love the boy. He told Peanut that he made sure only singles or married couples without kids rented in his buildings. Children were simply destructive. Lee believed that a group of children might literally tear a building to the ground or, at the least, wreak irreparable damage.

Why don't you move into one of my buildings? My best building. I have an apartment for you.

Now, you know I can't afford to live in one of your buildings.

Rent free, of course.

Well, I thought you don't low no kids in your buildings.

Of course, I'll make an exception for you and Boo.

Ain't you sweet. She kissed Lee on the cheek.

How soon can you move?

Real soon. She laughed.

Lee laughed too.

But I don't want to live around no Section Eight tenants and whatnot. She was serious. Boo needs a wholesome environment.

Lee laughed. Hey, I don't deal with welfare cases.

Well, all right, then.

Why don't you move on the first of the month? That was two weeks away.

Bet.

Lee was determined to be a father to Boo, if for no other reason than to impress Peanut. That was one reason why he had questioned Peanut's habit of leaving Boo home by himself. (And, it dawned on him, all the nights he and Peanut were at the lounge, Boo was at home alone. And Boo was alone whenever she was working.) So, the previous night, he had suggested that they all go to the zoo.

Boo's never been to the zoo, she said.

What?

I said, Boo ain't never been to no zoo.

Well, let's take him.

Why?

It's not right that a kid's never been to the zoo.

What you mean, it not right?

I just mean that the zoo is somewhere every kid should go.

A zoo ain't got nothin but animals.

But kids like animals.

The zoo boring.

It's not boring. Kids like animals.

How you know?

Trust me. I know.

Just animals.

We'll go Sunday.

We sposed to be going to yo office Sunday.

We'll go to the zoo, then we'll go to the office.

Boo might not like the zoo.

He'll like it.

He better.

Lee bit his tongue. Tasted fire. Hey, we'll all go have dinner afterward.

That sound good.

I know a nice restaurant.

Sound real good. What next?

Well . . . let's go back to my place. Watch some movies. Play some games.

Yeah. Then we gon put Boo to bed. We gon talk.

Talk?

Yeah, talk.

Yes, we can talk.

You know, *talk*. Boy, you dense.

In his car, parked in a sleeve of shade, Lee sat remembering the previous night's conversation. Thinking, *Yes, we will talk.* Something fine was going to happen to him today. He'd had enough of the past. Time to forget the dead. Time to start dealing with live people. Lee started the car.

Underneath a thick yellow yoke of light, Peanut and Boo stood in front of the building where they lived. Peanut bright in a light blue summer dress and white pumps. Boo small, even for a seven-year-old. Looked more like a midget than a child. White cotton double-breasted suit. A red and white polka-dot tie. White loafers. A square house cut, like Lee's. Sharp. As bright as a fresh egg. A cute midget.

Hey, baby girl.

Hey, honey.

They touched lips.

Hello, Mr. Christmas, Boo said. He extended a tiny hand.

Lee chuckled. Took the hand into his own. Hello, Boo. Aren't you sharp today?

The boy squeezed Lee's hand. He had a powerful grip.

We must go to the same barber. Lee tried not to concentrate on the pain in his hand.

That's a real nice haircut you got, Peanut said. She kissed Lee on the cheek.

Thank you, Lee said. Ran his free hand over the privet hedge.

Boo didn't crack a smile. Yeah. We must go to the same barber, Mr. Christmas.

Lee tried to withdraw his hand.

That's a nice suit too, Peanut said.

Thank you, Lee said. His hand bubbled hot, deep in boiling water.

Boo withdrew his grip. Lee thought he had exaggerated the child's strength. Still, there was no denying the throbbing in his hand. The sun glowed brighter, spreading a fan of light. Boo's eyes, large and black, shining black. Lee took Peanut by the arm. Led her to the car. Boo walked beside them. Lee held the door open for Peanut. She slid into the front passenger seat. Lee shut the door quietly behind her. Held open the rear door for Boo.

Thank you, Mr. Christmas, Boo said.

You're welcome, Boo. Lee's hand throbbed.

I like yo car, Mr. Christmas.

Thank you, Boo. Lee shut the door behind the boy. Stepped quickly around the rear of his car. Opened his door and stooped into the driver's seat. We gon have a fine time today. He hit the ignition. The engine gurgled, then spit to life.

Gon do my best, honey, Peanut said. She smiled. More pleasant than usual. Lee gave her a long look. Round face and a small mouth and freckles like seeds on both cheeks. Hair dyed to match her skin complexion. Combed forward into a pouf to expose the back of her neck. Her smile helped ease Lee's tension. It even made his hand feel better. But some feeling flowed up from his belly in soft surges. Wet his chest.

Better keep yo eyes on the road, Peanut said.

Lee swallowed. I got eyes all over my body.

I just bet you do.

Lee put both hands on the wheel. Eased up on the gas. Pulled the car into the middle of the road.

The sun roared without pause. This sun is something else today, Lee said.

Yeah, it is sort of bad, Peanut said.

Is that sun bothering you, Boo? Lee asked.

I'm all right, Mr. Christmas. The voice rose from the backseat.

I don't know how you can stand this sun, Lee said to Peanut.

Is that all you gon talk about? The sun?

Even Boo can't stand the sun. Lee watched the child's reflection in the rearview mirror. The cute midget sat stiff and straight, hands folded in his lap, legs dangling over the edge of the seat. Eyes closed to the sun.

He didn't say that, Peanut said. God. I don't want to hear bout no sun.

Okay, Lee said. The sun bothered him.

Peanut looked into the mirror. The sun don't bother Boo. He just meditating like a lil ole man and whatnot. He always do that.

Well, he sho is a quiet one. Lee frowned into the sun.

You ain't give him chance to say nothing yet. You keep talkin bout the sun.

I'm sorry. Here he was, apologizing in his own car.

Boo ain't quiet.

Lee looked in the mirror. Boo still had his eyes closed. I don't see how you can say that.

Look. He jus stoical.

What?

Boy, you dense. He stoical and whatnot.

Run that by me again.

Peanut rolled her eyes. Boy, I tell you. Boo like a lil ole man. Ain't cried but once in his life, and that was when he was born.

I don't believe that, Lee said. He couldn't explain why he didn't believe it.

Look, I'm tellin the truth. The only other time he cried is when I whupped him with a extension cord.

You hit him with an extension cord?

That's right.

But he's just a child.

Yeah, that's right, but I tore his butt up too. Didn't I, Boo? She glanced back over her seat.

Yes, ma'am. Boo didn't open his eyes.

He wasn't actin right, and I tore his butt up. You got to discipline yo kids.

Lee didn't say anything. He didn't want Peanut to get angry.

And let me tell you something. When Boo got circumcised, he didn't bat an eye. And weren't but two, three, months old.

Lee found this hard to believe. I once saw a ghost, he thought. Why do I find this so hard to believe? The doctors must have had him sedated, he said.

They don't sedate babies when they get circumcised and whatnot.

Who told you that?

Everybody know that. Anyway, nobody had to tell me. Seen it for myself. I had to watch. I wasn't gon let no doctor hurt my baby.

Why would a doctor want to hurt a baby?

Boy, you don't know nothing. Doctors are sadists.

Lee had to force his laughter back down his throat. Now, come on, Peanut, he said.

Don't you know anything about doctors?

I guess not.

Anyway—

She missed Lee's sarcasm.

—Boo jus like a lil ole man. One time I gave him a whupping wit a belt, and he jus looked up at me and said, Mamma, see if you can't whup me a little harder.

Lee considered the likelihood of this.

And he won't go to bed at night until he had a good whupping. Ain't that right, Boo? She glanced back over her seat.

Yes, ma'am. He didn't open his eyes.

I be so tired from whupping him, I just fall across the bed and go to sleep.

He ain't normal, Lee said. It had slipped out. He mentally slapped himself.

What you mean, he ain't normal?

Lee could feel her eyes burning a hole in the side of his face. I mean . . . he's special. Gifted.

That's right. He do real good in school. He always thinkin. Sometime he be jus as quiet as a Buddha on a shelf and whatnot.

I see.

They reached Turtle Avenue. Lee turned onto it.

Hey, pull up over at the sto. She pointed to Cut Rate Liquor half a block away. I need to put in some lottery numbers.

I didn't know that you played the lottery, Lee said.

Of course. Pull over.

Okay. Lee drove past the store.

You passed up the sto and whatnot, Peanut said.

I'm going to get that spot over there in the shade.

Are you talking bout the sun again?

No. I just want to get a shady spot.

You and yo shade.

Lee drove half a block past the store and parked in a space beside a tree. Disappointed to discover that it did a poor job of blocking the sun. Its leaves few and thin, the space between them like the space between the spokes of a wheel. They mainly dropped over the sidewalk.

What's yo birthday? Peanut asked.

What?

Silly, I'm gon play yo birthday.

Oh. Ten five . . . You guess the rest.

Ain't you Mr. Secretive.

That's me.

Boo, keep Mr. Christmas company while I'm gone.

Fear moved inside Lee's chest.

Yes, ma'am, Boo said. He didn't open his eyes.

Peanut kissed Lee on the cheek. He didn't feel comfortable kissing in front of the kid. Had actually shivered when Peanut kissed him. He hoped that she didn't sense his uneasiness. Peanut got out of the car. Shut her door. To show her that he was at ease with himself, confident, Lee leaned over the passenger seat and called after her through the car window. Hey.

She halted and looked back at him over her shoulder.

Your caboose is shaking.

She smiled. It's sposed to shake. She moved on to the store.

Lee's fear died just that quickly, heart dancing inside his chest. He straightened up in his seat. That's some mamma you got there, Boo. He looked at the child's reflection in his rearview mirror.

Boo opened his eyes. They were black sunlight. Closing his eyes had drawn more sunlight into them. You likes my mamma, Mr. Christmas? Boo said. His face offered the same blankness, the same cold solitude.

I likes yo mamma a whole lot, Boo. The sunlight dripped through the leaves and plopped against the windshield.

Are you going to marry my mamma, Mr. Christmas?

I hope so, Boo.

Are you going to be my new daddy, Mr. Christmas?

Yes, Boo. I really want to.

Is my name gon be Goodwin Christmas?

I hope so.

I don't like that name.

Lee tried to avoid the child's eyes in the mirror's reflection. It's a nice name, Boo.

How'd you get a name like Christmas?

Well—

Do you know Santa Claus?

What?

Is Santa Claus yo brother, Mr. Christmas?

My name has nothing to do with—

Do you know Rudolph the Red-Nosed Reindeer?

Lee didn't know what to say.

Is Mr. Reindeer yo daddy?

Now, I told you, my name doesn't—

Do you know Frosty the Snowman?

I think I see yo mamma coming, Boo, he lied.

Does Frosty have a cold dick?

Where did you learn to talk like that? Lee gave Boo a fierce stare in the mirror. The child just looked him dead in the eye.

Does Santa Claus have a big dick?

Boo, keep your mouth closed until you mamma—

Do you want to see my big dick, Mr. Christmas? The child leaned back into his seat. The leather stretched beneath him. He unzipped his pants. Lee clutched his own chest. The child had ripped it open. He could feel the glare of sunshine gathering in his heart.

If you take that out of yo pants, I'll chop it off. But the child continued to finger inside his fly.

Why you getting frantic, Mr. Christmas?

Open yo mouth again, and I'll put my fist in it.

Chill, Mr. Christmas.

Lee spun in his seat and lunged for the child. Boo was quick. Dived beneath Lee's arms and onto the floor of the car. Lee couldn't reach the child. The steering wheel was clamping down at the point above his knees, preventing any further leverage. The child's tiny hand reached for the door handle. Lee worked back into the seat, but the child opened the door and crawled out of the car and onto the sidewalk before Lee could get his own door open.

Catch me if you can, Mr. Christmas. His underwear stuck out like a white thumb from his open fly. He took off running down the street, cutting a blazing path away from Cut Rate Liquor. Lee set off behind him.

Help! Mommy! the child screamed, dodging between waists and legs like some midget football player.

Lee ran in the street to avoid the crowded sidewalk. The sun loomed high. Lee wiped sweat from his brow.

Help! Rape! Stranger danger!

If anything happened to the child, Lee would have no chance with Peanut.

Stranger danger! People began to stop and look at Lee. He wanted the child. Sweat poured from his house cut—as if a water hose were concealed in his hair—and stung his eyes. A ball of terror had knotted up inside Lee's chest. People were watching him. Child molester! a woman screamed. He was certain she was chasing him. Boo cut around the corner of an alley as if jerked by a string. Lee took one long step and lunged onto the sidewalk. Two more steps took him around the corner of the alley. The sun dropped a cube of light that slammed into Lee. Lifted him into the air. An arch of wind pulled him back toward the earth. The cube roared back into the clouds. Lee felt nothing when he hit the ground, but his head falling backward.

Flat on his back, he caught sight of two bright eyes that he recognized as Boo's. The child stood above Lee, staring down into Lee's face. Blood on the cuffs of Boo's white pants. Blood on his tiny shoes. Lee figured that the blood was his own.

Why you put that on my shoes? Boo asked. His eyes deep and black and filled with sunlight. Something else sparkled there too.

Lee tried to speak.

Why you put that on my shoes? Gon, get up.

Lee tried.

Gon, get up. Why you put that on my shoes?

Tears fell from Boo's eyes. The sunlight was draining the eyes. Globes of light spilled into the blood on Boo's shoes. In Lee's vision, the shoes swam circles. Red fish.

The Near Remote

The police superintendent sat bent forward at his sturdy mahogany desk, a big man in a big leather armchair, framed by a floor-to-ceiling window looking out onto the vast and vicious wonders of the city. He was reading a file that lay flat upon the leather-topped surface of his desk, the tip of one finger inserted between a thin gold necklace and a massive mound of throat, the necklace like some faint and forgotten residue, ring around the collar. The finger slid, pendulum-like, to his left earlobe, paused there, swung back to his bulging Adam's apple, paused again, passed on to the other earlobe, paused still again, then lobbed back to the Adam's apple, only to reenact the full arc of motion.

Ward slammed the door shut.

The police superintendent raised his eyes from the file and saw menace, tall and bony, standing in his office. If he was surprised that someone had been watching him—and who knew for how long—he did not let on. He withdrew the hyperactive finger from under the gold necklace, wet his thumb against the blotter of his tongue, picked up the file between wet thumb and dry forefinger, and placed it on top of a stack of papers at the corner of the desk. He curled his small and enormously pink lips into a smile, placed both palms against the desk edge, and scooted his chair backward. Then he gripped the padded armrests, raised himself up from the seat, and came around the desk—carpet muffling the sound of his steps, white cordovans shining with a high polish—over to where Ward stood with a hand extended in welcome.

"Ward," he said. He spoke the single word to identify the man before him, as if he found it fully appropriate. "You've decided to come."

"I decided to come," Ward said. "I had to see you for myself."

"Pleased to have you with us." Hand extended, the police superintendent maintained his cordial and professional tone, either failing to detect or choosing to ignore Ward's rebuff.

Ward stuck a finger inside his nose and worked it around, some food-craving scavenger scrounging up the last helpings of a jelly jar. Only then did he offer to shake his other's hand. The police superintendent looked at the finger, looked Ward straight in the face. Ward seized one cuff of the police superintendent's white linen shirt—so out of season, the thinnest fabric in the coldest weather—and cleaned the mucus-covered finger on the sleeve, back and forth in slow even strokes, as if buttering a bread slice.

The police superintendent looked at the sleeve, and he stood there looking at it for quite some time. Through need and want Ward could not refrain from believing that he had succeeded in stripping away the man's studied veneer and that he was now actually witnessing some other life form taking shape, restructuring the flesh. But, to Ward's regret, the police superintendent slowly raised his line of sight and offered Ward a face lacking any signs of anger or distress or revulsion, a face that betrayed no emotion, just the attitude of authority and duty, and he spoke to Ward in polite even tones, asking that he be seated, motioning to a leather armchair directly in front of his desk. Cautiously, Ward settled into the chair. The police superintendent walked over to a second picture window and stood looking out, dust drifting like unmoored astronauts in two smoky shafts of sunlight on either side of him, while Ward projected acts of destruction onto the broad screen of the man's white-shirted back.

"A damn nice secretary you have," Ward said.

The police superintendent seemed to be looking off at a skyscraper, surprisingly small and dull in the afternoon sun. A heavy man, so heavy that he might at any moment fall through the floor and plunge forever downward.

"'Go right in.' Damn nice. It can't be easy for her."

The police superintendent made slow steps away from the window, toward his desk, then sat down leisurely in his big leather armchair, eyes trained on the desk, giving Ward time to study the lumpy mass of his head, to penetrate the armored skin and gaze into the black skull, where a dry cloud hovered, the gathered force of will, reason, and worry. Light from the window gave the desk a liquid glow, an ashtray floating there like a water lily. The police superintendent pushed his long thick fingers into the leather desktop—worms burrowing into black earth, the material stretching and squeaking—then joined the fingers of both hands in a meaty cup. He cleared his throat.

"Might we get to it."

Ward said nothing, his seeking gaze ranging over the police superintendent's oddly constructed face. A diminishing crop of brown hair. Small brown eyes under an overhang of heavy eyelids and thick brows, so deeply embedded that they seemed to be sinking into the quicksand of fat-headed flesh. A swollen church bell of a nose. A broad yard of chin. And large ears that flapped in butterfly-like delight at the slightest movement.

The police superintendent lifted his eyes to Ward's face. "I cannot stress enough"—gesturing with his hands—"how important it is that we follow our plan to the letter"—his palm held upward in supplication—"unless you can adduce any legitimate grounds for some fresh course of action." He locked his fingers before him on the desk.

Ward watched him in silence.

"I am sorry. Profoundly sorry. Every one of us should be entitled to a private corner in the garden." The police superintendent shook his head, weary, defeated. "Alas . . ." He parted his hands, nothing to offer.

Ward wet his lips. "The wonder of it," he said. "Your face takes me back. Alluvial. Ah, the joys of evolution."

The lines in the police superintendent's face grew tight, as if disparate threads of yarn had been yanked all at once. "If your associates had been more careful in their actions, perhaps we could—"

"My associates?"

"Yes. Speaking plainly."

"Allow me a question."

The police superintendent spoke no reply, watching Ward with a look of come-what-may.

"Did you by any chance spend your beloved lunch hour bobbing for ripe, juicy turds?" Just like that. He began unbuttoning his black overcoat.

The police superintendent watched the unbuttoning without comment, blinking each time a button snapped free. He stirred heavily in his seat, then pushed himself up from his chair and walked to a third massive window, his profiled face metallic and gray in skyscraper glitter, his gold necklace no longer visible to the casual or curious observer, safe under the depths of his collar. He extended his arm stiffly out in front of him as if preparing to bend it in salute, caught the soiled shirt cuff between the thumb and forefinger of his other hand, unsnapped the button, then rolled the sleeve up his arm—dense wiry hair on the wrist, now the forearm—to the elbow. He did the same with the other sleeve. Stood still a moment with his arms hanging at his sides. Then he brought both hands to his chest and pulled violently at his shirt like some high-story flasher exhibiting himself to the world, buttons catapulting into air. He twisted backward and began freeing himself of the shirt—thin gold necklace, bare heavy shoulders, bare meaty back and arms—tilting his torso to one side, then the other, until both sleeves were free. That done, he crumpled up the shirt between both hands, his violent belly hanging like a mound of descending lava over his belt, and moved forward, the sausage rolls of his sides quivering with each step and the shirt trailing along the carpet behind him. He dropped the garment into a wicker wastebasket and resumed his station behind his desk, hands folded in his lap, watching Ward with murderous hatred.

Ward gripped the arms of his chair and scooted to the edge of the seat, face extended over the desk, in breathing distance. Immobilized, the police superintendent continued to glare at him, even as the sun began to suddenly shift its position, a spotlight pivoting around the police superintendent until it took up a new station, where it beamed down at him from a furious angle and fired his face, bricklike in ever-brightening colors. This police superintendent, singled out for illumination, his chest rising and falling, crashing waves on his chest. After some time, his posture eased, his shoulders relaxed. He cupped his hands underneath his belly and began rocking in the chair, his nose hairs visible one moment, gone the next, visible, gone, and so on.

"As you know, in this suspect we are dealing with a man who has been fortunate enough to travel in some of our most distinguished circles, not to mention the"—he stroked hairs curling out of his chest like barbed wire—"access he has—"

"I've been thinking," Ward said.

At these words, the police superintendent rocked to a halt and fixed his gaze on Ward.

"Would you take my hand in marriage?"

The police superintendent grabbed the edges of the desk and leaned in close. "Look! I am appealing to your—"

"Don't refuse me."

"—better nature." His nostrils blew hot air into Ward's face. "A selfless act. Lives in the balance. After all, you gain as well. Your time to shine."

"So thoughtful of you. Such abundance of caution and concern."

The police superintendent poised over his desk, staring at Ward, indignation, abhorrence, annihilation.

It was cold where he lay, and under his head was a cold pillow. The yellowed glow of streetlamps seeping under and around the edges of the window shade, frail wisps of light spinning like ballet dancers in the dark, with a reserved wind tapping modest applause against the paned glass. He shut his eyes and let the world spin free. The next thing he knew, he had spun out of orbit, his brain ricocheting off the black walls of his skull. He opened his eyes and found darkness in slow dissolution.

"Everything all right in there?" A hand pounded muffled words into the door. He turned the cold pearl of his pillowed face in the direction of the sound. Still no visual evidence that the door even existed, but he knew it was there, shadows crawling—black crabs— in the strip of light under its frame.

He listened to the wet whine of the rusty radiator. Snuggled under the covers, nose-deep in layered warmth, peeking over the top quilt at the shadowed ceiling.

"Hey!"

"Just relax."

"The police superintendent will be here soon."

"Just relax." He turned back the bedcovers. Shivered to a cold greeting of air. Kicked his feet out from under the sheets. Sat upright in the bed—a cot, really, a narrow iron frame, small and set low—lax springs sagging under his insignificant weight. Placed his feet on the cold wooden floor. Seeing the thin window shade aglow with faint illumination, he tried unsuccessfully to convince himself that he felt its warmth on his skin. He bent forward and fingered the shade, which snapped back up on its roller, allowing morning light to rush into the room like a gate crasher—he shut his eyes.

"Hey!"

The shade spun and flapped. Some comfort in its sound.

"Relax. I'll be right out." He opened his eyes and reached up and pulled the shade, and a measure of darkness, down to its proper place. The window was completely frosted. Impossible to see through. He crossed his arms tightly about his chest and trembled as he stood. Circled the bed, arranging the bedcovers—folding ends, tucking edges, patting surfaces smooth. Removed two small plastic freezer-storage bags from the nightstand drawer, angled the fingers of one hand, then the other, inside each bag—translucent mittens—and lined the insides of his leather loafers, which were stationed on the seat of a wooden chair, the one black suit he owned draped over the chair back. He set the shoes on the floor between the chair legs. Rubbed his fingers diligently and carefully over a spot on the blazer's collar. Satisfied, he folded the suit across his forearm and carried it over to the closet, where he squatted and took his thermal underwear and wool socks from a cardboard box positioned in a corner, with two additional suits, one brown, the other dark blue, hanging above it. He set the several items of clothing on the chair, removed the top blanket from the bed, wrapped the blanket around his shoulders, smoothed the bedcovers, and exited the room with the clothing bunched against his chest.

Hands shoved in his pockets, a young officer who had spent the entire night outside Ward's door—his guardian, his warden—sat slumped over on a stool wearing his department-issued cap and jacket, the side of his young face barely visible in sixty-watt gloom. He turned his head and peered up at Ward, one corner of his mouth twisted as if he were biting down on something. The sight of Ward changed the look in his eyes, the angle of his chin, the red polish of his cheeks. He pulled his hands from his pockets, sat as straight as he possibly could on the stool, and redirected his gaze to a neutral wall.

Ward pulled one side of the blanket tighter about his shoulders. "Fine job," he said.

The young officer remained perfectly still, like someone sitting for a photograph, though Ward detected a faint suggestion of some forbidden emotion rising into his face.

Some time later, Ward came down the hall in sock feet, fully dressed otherwise, with the blanket shawled (sprawled warmth) around his shoulders; he was saddened to discover the young officer still at his post outside his room, now leaning forward on the stool, hands stuffed inside his pockets, head bowed, teeth chattering. For a moment Ward's hands and legs refused to carry him forward, his thoughts spiraling around him in dark constricting bands. Before long he was able to move close enough that, if he so chose, he could offer a full sentence or two of consolation and support. However, his thoughts were soft in his wet insides like the tissues of coral but petrified when they hit the air. He settled on putting a firm hand on the officer's shoulder, a touch that altered the crumpled tone of the other's body.

Ward entered the room, dismayed to find the police superintendent stretched out on his cot, arms folded, pretzel-like, behind his head—not unlike how Ward himself might have been positioned in times past, less somber days—the mattress sagging under him, white bottom almost touching the dark floor, and the high sack of his belly like some missile preparing for launch through the ceiling. His breathing, a labored wheezing, did not come easy, some beached sea creature. He adjusted himself, turning slightly, bedsprings straining and squeaking. It was only then that Ward saw a white derby adorning his windowsill, drawing attention like some ill-placed trophy.

He stood there, astounded. "Glad you see fit," he said.

The police superintendent turned his head and looked Ward up and down, disgusted, an action of such surprising force that Ward's lips parted like a budding flower, shocked air pushing through, the bones in his legs starting to crumble and powder.

"Have a seat."

Ward collapsed into the chair beside the bed.

"Crazy damn hours."

"Don't blame me."

"No, I won't. I can send your friend a note of thanks and—"

"He's not my friend."

"Oh no? Then how would you describe him?"

Ward sat there watching his other.

"Please, hold nothing back. I wish to make every effort to understand."

Ward shrugged the shawl from his shoulders, onto the chair back, and bent forward in the chair, the plastic-lined shoes at his feet. "There's nothing to understand."

"No?"

"No." Ward tugged and pulled at the tongue of one shoe as he began to squeeze and wiggle and stomp his foot inside it.

"Indeed. Not surprising, your curious—"

"Why don't we just go?"

"—range of reasoning."

"Kindly spare me the sermon."

"Certainly. They don't pay me to preach. What would you care to hear? You would care to hear that—"

"We have someplace to go." He squeezed in the second foot and stood.

"No? Perhaps if I kneeled down and—"

"You wallow!"

The police superintendent popped upright on the bed. "Nothing could wallow like you." He sat there on the bed staring up at Ward, his still form merged with the coarse sheets, the iron cot, a carved figure leaning out in relief from the substance that contained it. The radiator popped and hissed in the silence.

"Are we going to sit here all day?"

"May you rot."

"Take comfort in the thought." Ward lifted his overcoat from its closet hook and slipped inside it, his body mockingly insubstantial, the padded wrapping loose on his frame, like a hospital gown. But the police superintendent made no effort to move, anchored to stubborn place, unable to pull his hate back inside him link by link.

"Why don't I meet you downstairs," Ward said.

These words might have gone unheard or escaped comprehension. It was only when Ward started for the door that the police superintendent took to his feet and blocked his exit. He smacked his palms against his trouser legs to rid them of lint, shook the lapels of his overcoat, and brushed his hair flat with the sides of his hands. Then he eased around Ward, lifted his white derby from the windowsill, and fitted it onto his head. He pulled the door open—he did not hurry—and motioned for Ward to go through.

The winter sky was high and clear above short snowbanked streets. White wonder, enormous pancakelike flakes falling to the earth in rapid succession, blown aloft again in fierce twirlings. A car idled in fixed brilliance, all metal and glass. The hard-of-muscle young officer who'd guarded Ward's room tugged harder at Ward's elbow. Ward bent into the car and settled back onto the rear passenger seat. The officer slammed his door tight against the wind and cold, and in that instant, the front passenger door hinged open, snow rushing in with malicious intentions of beating the police superintendent to his seat. Only when his door slammed shut did he thoroughly examine his white derby for damage. The young officer took the other end of the rear passenger seat and shut the door. He turned his face to the glass, a full yard of leathered space between him and Ward. A second uniformed officer positioned himself behind the steering wheel and eased the smooth-running car forward. "Coldest day of the year," he said, black-gloved fingers drumming on the wheel.

Ward thought about what the gloves kept out and all that they kept in. Hoping to calm himself, he brushed snow from his coat, removed his own gloves, and blew hot air into the well of his joined hands. The wipers switched back and forth across the windshield like lascivious buttocks. A second car moved ahead of them, venting smoke. A third car behind.

"Coldest so far."

"You're a genius," Ward said. "Now turn up the goddamn heat."

"What?" The driver craned his neck to look back over the seat. Perhaps he would steer the car with one hand and shoot Ward with the other. "You want to repeat that?"

"You heard me."

"Officer," the police superintendent said, "do the honor. Turn up the heat."

The driver shot a quick unprotesting glance at his superior and clicked on the blower.

"Thanks, you cocksucker."

The police superintendent looked at Ward's reflection in the rearview mirror. "Take a moment or two, if you must."

Ward offered no reply, only sat rubbing his palms together. The blower roaring like an untamed beast.

"That warm enough for you?" the driver asked.

"No. Have your mother send up a fagot or two from hell."

The driver began rocking from side to side in his seat, his fingers tapping anxious rhythms on the steering wheel. The police superintendent gave him a sharp look, and he pressed his shoulders into his seat, the dark shape of his head looking straight ahead, through the snow-repellent windshield.

"Kiss him once for me, would you?" Ward said to the police superintendent.

The police superintendent turned around in his seat and gave Ward his familiar look of disgust. He shook his head slowly from side to side. "Who would have ever thought."

"Certainly not you."

The ride was otherwise uneventful, the streets specked with people, black forms silhouetted against the snow.

"Here"—the police superintendent dropped a ring of keys into Ward's lap, letting them fall from his hand with the highest form of disregard, a soiled-nose wipe—"the keys to the city."

"You're so thoughtful." Ward deftly deposited the keys into some inside pocket of his coat. He looked over and saw that the young officer who had kept vigil outside his door was snickering into his upturned jacket collar. When they made it to their destination, this same officer pulled Ward from the car and rudely bumped him and shoved him into the snow, but in such a way as to make the action seem accidental, an inadvertent trip over the curb. Ward regained his feet, brushed snow from his clothes, retrieved his scattered thoughts, and patted his pockets to be sure that the keys were still there, showing no concern that his outer garments were thoroughly soaked through. Then the police superintendent took a firm hold of Ward's gloved hand and led him forward as if he were a child on the first day of school. Black and slick, his streamlined shoes jumped above the snow, one after the other, like dolphins.

They had walked some fifty paces, Ward's breath coming a little harder with every step, when the police superintendent stopped as if on cue and spun Ward in front of him like a practiced dancer.

"Please sign, here and here."

Ward did as instructed. The police superintendent slipped the damp form into his jacket and stood before Ward under his white derby, the hat tiny on his massive head, like some ghastly baby bonnet. "I would be lying if I said it has been a pleasure."

"Spare me."

The police superintendent turned and headed back for his car and left Ward to the snow and wind. Ward vowed to take away with him some memory of the man. However, the weather being what it was, he was already having trouble remembering exactly how the man's features fit together. So much so that Ward considered calling out to him and requesting a quick but comprehensive physical inventory, fully aware that, in all likelihood, the police superintendent would not acquiesce. But instead, he looked through the neutral and colorless distance and saw an old five-story walk-up building slanting away from the ground—a splinter angling up from skin—at a precarious angle, snow swirling around the structure as if to lasso it upright. His appointed destination. What was keeping it standing? He turned a last time to look at the police superintendent, who was now leaning against the car—white derby snugly atop his head—where the two young officers were hunched over, sharing a cigarette. Uniformed men from supporting vehicles worked to cordon off the street with brass barricades they took from the trunks of their own cars, in a shared geometry of secrecy and isolation.

Ward reached into his coat pocket for the ring of keys but fumbled them against his chest into the snow. At once he dropped to his knees, biting at the ends of his gloved fingers until his hands were free of the leather. He stuck his bare fists into the snow and began clawing about—hungry bear or ice fisherman—reacting to the cold in an almost clinical way, the snow both surprising and mundane. He scooped up two fistfuls and weighed them in each palm, and he told himself that he would do better to avoid any new feelings and impressions he was not yet conscious of, which he had not possessed in years. However, his proximity to the earth allowed him to see that snow was actually rising up from the street and fleeing into the heavens—an impossible journey, as the domed sky would allow no escape. No sadness at the realization, for the thought took hold of him: at this very moment he was kneeling at the very center of the world, at its cold icy navel. He trembled to shake himself free.

Twenty feet ahead he spotted a familiar figure trudging through the snow toward him. He stuck his hands back into the slushy mounds and worked more frantically after the keys. Heard the snow-crunching approach of the two young officers behind him. Looked up and turned his head to see them bobbing forward with pistols drawn. Had they misinterpreted the direction and meaning of his submerged and sweeping hands, mistaking purposeful search for beckoning wave? He thought to shout, "The keys! I dropped the keys!" Burrowing down, trenched in this place, which had already started to corrode beneath him, melt and puddle around his knees.

The Green Apocalypse

The dead just ain't what they used to be.
– ROQUE DALTON

Down in the alley, Chitlin Sandwich sat wide-legged on a fifteen-speed racer, fifteen himself, a schoolboy, dressed like somebody's granddaddy, a wide fedora slanted across his face, his tall skinny frame entombed in a wide double-breasted blazer, a diamond pin centered in a fat red and green polka-dot tie, flashy argyle socks, peeking above two-tone patent-leather shoes, like two shiny puddles of mud beneath his cuffed and pleated baggy slacks. He was sipping from a can wrapped in a brown paper bag and drumming his fingers on a burlap newspaper sack that hung over one shoulder. Sheila was certain that the bike belonged to Hatch—her little brother—or that it was an exact replica, its twin. She pressed her face hard to the window glass and cut her eyes at him. He regarded her with frank indifference, as still as an owl. Then he tilted the bag and drank long and deep. She felt hot anger rising and spreading throughout her face, elongating fingers of flames. His diamond tie pin caught the sunlight. He took one final gulp, crushed the wrapped can like a mosquito between both hands, and sent it clattering over his shoulder, into an open trash barrel. He pulled a *Daily Chronicle* from the burlap sack, drew back his arm like a pitcher, only to toss the newspaper underhanded, like a softball. It soared in early-morning air and plopped like a dead bird onto Sheila's porch, inches from her window. A spasm of rage gripped her throat. I'm twenty-four and educated and the assistant human-resources manager at the growing East Shore Bank, and I will not put up with this. She went out onto the porch.

You're lucky that didn't hit my window, she said, fists clenched at her sides.

Ain't nobody tryin to hit yo window.

What are you doing here in the first place?

He narrowed his cunning eyes and grinned. Only later would she realize that this was the first time she had seen him mirthful in seven years. Can't you see? Here to delivery yo paper, baby.

Look, I don't play. She swallowed, breathing more easily now. If you want to play, go to a school yard.

His eyes flared up with hate.

Shoo, boy. Shoo! Her hands brushed at him, brushed him away, dirt.

He started off on the racer, his eyes looking back at her. I'll be seein you, ba-by! He blew her a kiss.

She exploded. Felt her hair singe and crackle. Boy, I'll slap the shit out of you! She started down the porch steps.

His eyes glinted with rage. Pedaling, bike and boy disappeared.

That's right. You better run.

She turned back up the steps and went into her apartment. Paced the room. In her anger, she had forgotten to confront him about the bike. She had purchased a red fifteen-speed Zurbo Turbo Urban Assault professional racer a week ago as a gift for Hatch when she learned that Lucky Green's Groceries had hired him as a delivery boy—his first job. She was excited that at age fifteen he had finally set his athletic-shoed feet on the road to maturity. Now Chitlin was riding the bike.

She halted. Composed herself for work. One must be prompt. She moved into the bedroom, checked herself in the mirror, liked what she saw. Long black braids with neatly spaced colored beads flowed away from her brown face, down to her nape, trawl lines on night water. A gray knee-length dress fit close on her tight and toned curves. I will marry when I find the right man. The thought died as suddenly as it had arisen.

She quit her apartment, secured all six locks, and descended scrubbed stone porch steps—feeling both nimble and heavy—as if drawn by some force beneath the grassy lawn. She made her way down a short cement path to a speared wrought-iron fence and gazed out at the quiet streets, geometric lawns and hedges, prim flats (like her own), and houses of North Shore—gazed, searching for signs of Chitlin Sandwich. Nothing stirred. Disappointed, she opened the fence, closed it firmly behind her, and walked the few feet to her lime-colored Datsun 280ZX. Got behind the wheel. She was tempted to search for Chitlin Sandwich, but the bank came first. The groan of ignition. She handled keys, gears, and buttons with the skill of an astronaut.

Eased the car onto the highway. Watched the road through the windshield, and the windshield watched her back. Thinking about her brother, buried reflections. Fifteen years ago, Mamma had gotten so disgusted with fat greedy chicken-eatin wing-robed preachers (with each word, shout, hum, and grunt of his Sunday sermon, Reverend Ransom had examined her with knowing eyes) that she stopped attending church altogether. A ghost began to plague her family. He would nibble Sheila's toes or fart above her bed—anything to prevent her from sleeping. She grew restless and dizzy. Bumped into objects like a spun cat. The ghost made comical faces whenever she sat on the toilet. But he soon tired of these games, tired of Sheila, and began to frequent Mamma at night, singing low-down blues all the while. (His blues-toned laughter still ruled her dreams.) Mamma found both prayer and potions ineffective. She sought the advice of her medium, who suggested that she change the direction of her bed. This worked. Then her belly began to round. Nine months later the ghost made a final appearance. He hot-wired a car, drove Mamma to the Cedar Sake Hospital, and set her down on the curb outside the emergency room. One hour later Hatch came quietly into the world.

You haven't finished them files yet? Petite, smooth, and beautiful, a fairy, Angela spoke from the opposite desk. Files were scattered over Sheila's desk like stones from a felled wall.

I'll have them done by the end of the week.

I hope so.

Yeah, girlfriend. Niece spoke from the desk to the right of Sheila. She was as dark as a tree trunk and just as round and promising. Angela on her left, Niece on her right, and Sheila trapped between them. Better hurry up. You only got two days.

Two days is plenty of time.

If you say so.

I say so.

She don't know what she sayin.

Sheila trained her eyes on an application and read it a third time.

You sure are sluggish this mornin, Angela said. Why you so slow this mornin?

Oh, that big strong long man musta kept her up last night.

Niece and Angela shared a foul laugh.

Lift both yall minds outta the gutter.

Nawl. Why don't you come down here wit us.

You wish.

The three women worked in silence for some time.

We're going to have dinner after the demonstration Saturday, Angela said. Maybe do some dancing.

Where?

Frank told me to ask you.

Let me think about it.

How bout the Sugar Shack? Niece suggested.

That new club?

Yeah. Dinner, dance, drinks, dudes. All a good girl need. Niece flicked her tongue fast and nasty.

The car rocked roughly over some potholes. Roofs lay in a crazy jigsaw against the sky. South Shore was a decent neighborhood, but Sheila searched long and hard to find a parking space in sight of Mamma's living room window. She roared into the spot like a professional test driver and quit the engine. All had gone well at work. Troubled, preoccupied, she wondered at the upheaval. Disorder. She had decided to visit Mamma and report the morning's events, even if her words fell on deaf ears.

She was about to place her key inside the lock of the front door, when she heard voices on the other side of the door. She stood quietly in the hall of the building and listened.

Now, I never minded yo playin guitar.

No, ma'am.

It kept you outta trouble and yo grades ain't never suffer. I didn't even mind yo going over this nigger's house to practice, cause I thought them other musicians might improve yo sounds. But I ain't gon let you play at no bar.

Please, Mamma. This my chance.

As God is my witness.

Please, Mamma. I'm beggin.

The only way you can go to that bar is by kickin my ass, and I don't think you qualified to do the job.

Mrs. Wardell—

It's Miss Wardell.

Miss Wardell, please allow me to interrupt. Salamanders is not a bar but a disco, and a prominent establishment, I might add. I can assure you that it is frequented by decent and well-educated individuals like yourself.

Please.

It is located in the East Shore area.

Mister, my son ain't but fifteen.

Yes. I can see how that might trouble you. But let me stress that I've been in the music business for fifteen years and have encountered few problems. The owner of the disco is a close friend of mine. He is a professional man like myself.

I thought you drive a truck.

I do. A fourteen-wheeler, but . . . Anyway, the owner understands the situation. He understands my concept. That is—

Let me ask you one thing.

Ma'am?

What kind of an establishment opens its doors to teenagers?

Not to contradict you, ma'am, but it doesn't open its doors to—

Hey.

Ma'am?

Let me ask you this.

But—

If you been in the music business fifteen years, how come you ain't a star? Where's yo video?

Ma'am, it's like this—

Concept, please.

I've lacked marketability. Now, Sound Productions has just that. Give me a moment, ma'am. You see, all of the members of my band are youngsters like your son. My engineer is also an enterprising young man. My own son is the drummer. Ma'am, do you think that I'd take my own son into any establishment where his life would be in danger?

Mamma said nothing for a time. Then: I tell you what. Hatch can go. But let me say one thing. If anything happens to him, I'm coming for you.

Hatch. You grown now. You defy my word. From now on you save all the money you make from yo route, and the next time you need a flanger or a phase shifter or octave divider or synthesizer or ring modulator or wah-wah pedal, or fuzz box, you better not ask me.

Don't do that, Mamma. At fifteen, Hatch was already taller than Sheila, equal in height to Chitlin Sandwich, equally thin, with big boyish ears and a hairless face.

Sheila. What you doin here?

Sheila smiled. They had not heard her key turn in the lock. She closed the door behind her. Oh, I'm jus droppin by.

Mamma watched her, unbelieving, perhaps. She was forty and gorgeous. Tall—a good five ten—she stood out in her nice dresses and clean stockings and decent pumps. She wore her hair pulled back in a ponytail to accentuate her large eyes and high cheekbones. Her smooth dark skin, full breasts, small waist, big butt, and shapely legs drew comment. She thanked anyone who complimented her, even scandalous men. Sheila thought to kiss her but decided against it. Never kiss her when she's mad. Never.

I was jus talkin to yo brother here. Hardheaded.

No, I ain't, Mamma.

He think he grown now.

No, I don't.

Go on and be grown. She spoke into Hatch's face. And spend yo grown money.

Mamma—

Sheila saved her money when she was yo age.

Both Mamma and Hatch looked at Sheila for support. Sheila said nothing.

Go on, Mr. Grown, with yo grown self.

Please, Mamma—

I said all I'm gon say. Come on, Sheila. Help me wit dinner.

I'll be right there. She waited until Mamma went into the kitchen. Mamma on yo case, huh?

Word.

She'll calm down.

I hope so. Crestfallen, doomed, Hatch watched the floor.

Cheer up. She'll change her mind.

Hatch said nothing.

She was secretly satisfied with Mamma's tough stand—was it enough, and would it halt what was already in motion?—but she was careful not to show it. Guess who I saw today?

Who?

Chitlin Sandwich.

Hatch continued to watch the floor.

And you know what else?

What?

He was riding your bike.

Hatch raised his head and looked her in the face with protesting eyes. It wasn't my bike.

Looked like it.

Couldn be. My bike's in there. Hatch pointed to the closed patio.

Sheila weighed his words. He was lying. She was sure of it. She could see it in his eyes.

A white Jaguar bounced and swayed through nervous traffic. Animate ill will. Chitlin's wrath seemed to buoy him. Bent and cramped, he floated in the space between steering wheel and hood. A relic. His mouth wide, almost too broad for his skinny face.

Her rearview mirror drummed with the sight. Witness, her eyes recorded, vision hurrying like venom through her body. She gunned the engine with a hoarse roar, turned at the corner, turned again, made several more turns, until she was back where she had started. Car, boomerang. She curved to the curb. Engine running, she sat, quiet, behind the wheel. Her head was numb. Lost him. So now he's following me? Okay, I got something for him. Wait and see. He'll think twice about messin wit me.

■ ■ ■

Boy, what's wrong wit you? Roused from sleep, in her yellow house-coat with white flowers, Mamma watched Hatch from her reclined position on the couch, the cords in her neck tense, as if straining to contain airbound blood. Her red-house-shoed feet crossed. Ashy ankles like gray fish eyes. Lips puckered from toothless gums. She'd lost her teeth as a child in the Sippi South, when a reckless car struck her on a lonely dirt road. Specialists fashioned her a new set, which she had a hard time keeping track of. Once she'd left them on a friend's dashboard and dispatched an embarrassed Sheila to retrieve them. Speak up. She switched her gaze to Sheila for a moment, the eyes like stones, scraping Sheila's skin.

Head down, Hatch cried without wiping his eyes, tears running. A swelling reddened his brow, a small red knob. He attempted to speak between sobs, bubbled words and saliva.

Boy, speak up.

Chitlin Sandwich bit me wit a sock.

What?

Chitlin Sandwich hit me wit a rock.

Mamma continued to look at him, letting the wet revelation soak in. Her eyes slowly found Sheila's face. She had been put in charge of Hatch. They shared a two-bedroom apartment—she and Mamma, one bedroom; Hatch the other—on the top floor of a three-story brick courtyard building, broad high picture window overlooking the Stonewall Projects, a single playground the center of three seven-story steel high-rises that bloomed into city sky. Flecks of waste. Free-floating rage. It was Mamma's desire to spirit out of the neighborhood first chance.

Mamma rose from the couch, shuffled into the kitchen, house shoes slapping the bare floor, and returned with two potsherds. She took Hatch's hand and raised it, palm upward, beggar-fashion. Placed the potsherds inside. Don't let the serpent of hatred rise in yo heart, she said, but I want you to go back out there and bust that Chitlin Sandwich side his head.

No, ma'am. Hatch was eight, and tall for his age—threatening, even—but he was clumsy (Mamma forbade him to handle delicate objects) and gentle, and would wrap crooked Band-Aids around the broken wings of dragonflies. He would thank Mamma when she whupped him—her blows and words synchronized, his body jerking to avoid the rhythmic belt—and promise to do better.

You back-talkin me?

No, ma'am.

Then get out there and do what I told you to do.

I would prefer not to.

What? Get! She shoved him, stumbling, out the door. Stood looking at Sheila. What are you standing there for? Go wit him.

It was a day of filtered sunshine, half-cloud, half-sun. Chitlin Sandwich waited before the gray mass of the building. Chitlin Sandwich, waiting. Dark, red, sparkling, the child of unmothering and unfathering deeps. Anyone even remotely connected with the Abraham Lincoln Elementary School knew that his mamma dressed him from the Goodwill. She ran the streets in glossy hip huggers, a new man on her arm every week, and she aided and supported two grown brothers, Snake and Lake, criminals in hiding, pursued. She cooked every Sunday and used the leftovers for the remainder of the week. Her specialty was the chitlin sandwich: chitlins on white bread with hot sauce, onions, lettuce, pickles, and tomatoes. Chitlin rose a full three inches over the tallest kid in the neighborhood. (Perhaps the sandwiches fed his strange growth and behavior.) Feared, he was also called upon, since he instinctively understood electronics. He could repair a toaster and a computer, a television and a cellular phone, with equal ease. Word had it he never used tools.

Chitlin walked, the hinged arms and legs of a cardboard Halloween skeleton. Hatch closed his eyes and whirled both potsherds. One caught Chitlin—he made no attempt to defend himself—squarely behind the earlobe. Hatch opened his eyes to red sight. He ran back into the courtyard. Halted beside Sheila. She knew what he was thinking: stand his ground or answer to Mamma.

Chitlin crossed the street for Stonewall, blood trickling between fingers stopping his wound. He did not hurry. Steady and calm. Sheila watched from the courtyard, drawn by the clean power of curiosity. She had never seen such stoicism and determination in a child. She caught one last glimpse of him before Stonewall swallowed him.

Did you see that? she said.

See what?

Did you see that?

He bleedin. He gon beat me up.

You didn't see it? As her brother's fear weighed on her, Chitlin Sandwich reappeared, walking with swift firm steps, dragging with one hand some object that scraped the concrete behind him like a fallen muffler. She held up one hand to block the sun so that she could see better, but there was no light to block. Sight improved as he came closer. She felt a violent knocking in her stomach, neither fear nor anger. Comic disbelief.

That Chitlin Sandwich got a sword.

What?

Look.

The sword was better than three feet long, the dark brown handle embedded with tiny red stones like mosquito bites. The blade itself was even sicker, with pockets of rust like sores on a mangy dog. Boy and sword were less than a yard away now. She burst out in a spasm of giggles.

Look at that ole silly sword!

Hatch tripped over his own feet making it behind her. He encircled her waist with his arms and hugged her tightly. He gon cut me up! Don't let him cut me up. I'm sorry, Chitlin! He peeped out from around her waist.

Let me go. She tried to shake him loose. Couldn't. He ain't gon cut nobody.

Using both hands Chitlin raised the sword above his head like a sledgehammer and brought it wildly down onto the sidewalk. She was too swift, even with Hatch hugging her waist. A taste of gall rose up inside her. She pried Hatch loose. Chitlin readied the sword. She ran right up to him and punched him in the face. He fell straight backward, a domino, and narrowed the concrete.

The sword fell. Clanged. Nothing moved. Silence. Time.

Why you hit my baby! A lady under a helmet of pink curlers was running toward Sheila from across the street. She moved with incredible speed, flabby thighs bouncing and balancing on skinny bird calves. Why you hit my baby! Black dots peeped through her faded green T-shirt—cut above the navel—and pubic hair crept up her belly over blue jean shorts, panty small and tight.

Yo, Slim, someone yelled. People were hanging out windows, watching from the playground.

Tell her, Shorty.

Yall, get it on.

Party time.

You ain't got no business puttin yo hands on my child, the bird-slut said, close now.

How'd you like me to punch you?

You ain't gon punch nobody.

Sheila looked over her shoulder. Mamma. Malice. Still and angry in red house slippers, her hand on something inside the pocket of the flowered housecoat. She'd snapped in her dentures. Hatch was gripping her free hand with both of his.

Hey, there go another bitch.

This should be good.

Word.

Gon, party, ladies.

The bird-slut fixed Mamma with a hard cold squint. Mamma

watched her back. Chitlin Sandwich managed to raise himself on shaky legs. Then he dropped back to the sidewalk, cartoonlike, as if his bones had been liquefied.

The bird-slut trained her eyes on him.

Sheila, get yo behind over here.

Sheila obeyed Mamma's order.

Mamma and the bird-slut stood there, eternally, it seemed, and traded cold stares, eyes flicking.

I don't think no hittin will be necessary, Mamma said.

Mother Chitlin made no response.

I tell you what: since our children can't play together, we gon keep them apart.

Fine wit me. The bird-slut leaned from one thin leg to the other.

Mamma eyed Hatch. Now, he ain't gon play wit you, and if I find you playin wit him, I'm gon beat yo ass.

Yes'm.

Chitlin, get up from there.

Now, if he bother you, come see me.

Yes'm.

Chitlin!

In one motion Chitlin Sandwich arced to his feet, fast and stiff, like a stepped-on broom.

Get yo sword.

He retrieved the sword.

Mamma stiffened. Hatch lowered his head. Chitlin staggered over to the bird-slut, his shirt collar soaked with blood. He watched Sheila, his powerful will packed into his stare.

You heard what she said. The bird-slut eyed him, her voice unfaltering. He ain't gon play wit you, and you ain't gon play wit him. Find you some new friends.

Chitlin watched Sheila. The slut snatched him around. They started across the street, the sword dragging behind, sparks showering, crowd parting. He swirled round on one foot and shook his fist at Sheila, slow and stiff. She rolled her eyes. The slut snatched him forward. He craned his bloody neck and threw his eyes back over his shoulder at Sheila. The bird-slut slapped him upside the head.

A week later Sheila watched the Stonewall playground through the all-knowing third story picture window. Swing set. Two small figures at either end. Vast space between them. Chitlin Sandwich swinging in one direction, Hatch swinging in the other. That thing is done, Mamma said. But, Mamma . . . I saw them. I—

Stop botherin me. That thing is done.

She braked suddenly to avoid tail-ending the car in front of her.

Hey, lady. Don't you know how to drive?

Do yo mamma! She cursed softly. Put her mean foot on the gas like the pedal was a roach. Jerk! Saying it out loud.

Bubbled in, she drove, all silence and substance. Random contact these past seven years. Casual mentions: Hey, you remember Chitlin Sandwich from the old hood? Well, I ran into him at . . . Oh, guess what. I bumped into Chitlin Sandwich at . . . Listen to this. I saw Chitlin Sandwich at . . . Easily explained, perhaps. (Similar circles: Hatch was a musician—he plunked away for hours at a time, his slow clumsy fingers moving on the strings like earthworms—and Chitlin a producer, an engineer, a technician, a stage manager, and a promoter, in local music circles, and the CEO of Green Wig Productions.) Easily explained but for recent signs denoting more.

Hatch on the corner. Awaiting her arrival. White Jaguar pulling away from the corner. Slow, taking its time . . . Hatch passing through a fenced-in (caged) basketball court. Shapely guitar case like a sarcophagus at his side. White Jaguar slowing down to greet him.

As in olden times, so now. But why had Chitlin Sandwich suddenly launched an open assault, after years of latent wickedness? Mindful of traffic, she snatched her cell phone and pinned it between her raised shoulder and slanted ear. The loud electric buzz

JEFFERY RENARD ALLEN

taunted her, raising doubt, mocking her effort. Should she call Mamma? Could she awaken her? Were her ears willing?

Hey, Mamma. It's me.

Hey, daughter.

What you doin?

Nothin. Jus gettin ready fo bed.

Where Hatch?

In there wit that guitar of his. I made him put on those head-phones. I ain't tryin to hear that noise.

He never stops.

Does a thief?

She is thinking about what to say. You know, I need to tell you something.

What's that?

Well, you know . . .

Go ahead.

It's very important. Very very important.

Jus tell me.

Well, Mamma . . . you got to do something about Hatch and that Chitlin Sandwich.

What?

You know, Chitlin Sandwich.

Who?

Chitlin Sandwich. You remember him. From Stonewall. Him and his nasty low-life mother.

Why are you bringing all that up?

Cause I saw—

I mean, that was a long time ago. How many years has that been now?

But you don't understand. I saw—

Didn't I say I'm through wit all that? Why can't you listen? Did I not say that I'm through wit all that?

Sheila hung up the buzzing powerless phone. It was a matter of great sorrow that Mamma could be so naive about the clandestine friendship between Chitlin and Hatch. Left to her care, Hatch's low-flaming soul would evaporate through his skin. She did not understand the resilient life of evil. Snakes keep a reserved set of fangs. But, given charge, she would set things right.

She honked a car from her path.

She was fording a river of steaming greens. Hard bacon, stone under her feet. She rose with the river. Air. She was a green wasp flying through sweet heat. She smoothly landed on a wide tree trunk. Disemboweled it with her stinger. Green viny guts exploded from the tree's solid interior like coiled toy snakes. Extended in all directions—trails, tracks, traces.

Advice from the wise: slice them pies.

Yeah. Get all you can get. And then some.

That's why Frank and I are saving all our money to open up this coffee shop. Angela licked a gum-backed stamp, then thumbed it onto a long envelope. It's gon be the bomb. Computer surfing. High-speed internet and an iPod room. Virtual-reality room. Game room. DVD room. Pool room. Chess room. You name it. And a good old-fashioned coffee shop and some slammin good coffee.

Sounds good, Sheila said. She grabbed a file and spread its contents on the desk before her.

You should invest.

I'll think about it. Let me think about it.

I'll invest, Niece said.

You ain't got no money.

Niece grinned, proud.

I don't believe it, Sheila said. Sight surprised.

What?

He wouldn't.

What?

No!

Girl, what?

Out in the main banking area, a teller passed Chitlin Sandwich a stack of crisp bills across a marble counter. Have a nice day. Smiled. He did not move from the window. He stood counting the bills, slow and careful.

Chitlin Sandwich.

Chitlin who?

Where?

Counting done, he slipped the bills inside his blazer, near his heart. Turned and saw Sheila and the other two women watching him. He walked in their direction, casual and unconcerned.

He better not!

Who?

What's going on?

He stopped before the glass door that opened into their office and stood there sullenly, watching Sheila. He was so tall that he would need to stoop under the door frame to enter. His wide baggy suit could not hide his puny body. No muscle. His bones lay loosely in his flesh. He studied Sheila a moment longer and moved on.

Who was that?

Nobody.

Call him back, Niece said. He kinda cute.

Girl, can't you tell? He's jus a boy.

Don't matter to me. Them young boys never get tired.

You know him?

Not really. Sheila pulled up his account on her computer.

Girl, what you doing? You better finish those files.

I'll get to them. In a minute.

So, you still coming to the march Saturday? Angela snapped for the waiter.

Yes. Sheila veiled her knees with a green cloth napkin.

Good.

You know I'm coming, Niece said. And you better introduce me to some men. I like the political type.

Girl, please. A towel would get you wet.

Niece grinned. Proud.

The waiter arrived, leather-covered pad and pen at the ready. How are you ladies this afternoon?

Fine. Angela spoke for all of them.

Something to drink?

I'll take the house wine. White.

He wrote on his pad.

Me too, Niece said. Red.

And you, madam?

Zinfandel.

Had he asked Sheila a second or two later, she would have muttered *Shit*. Chitlin Sandwich was lunching—broiled lamb and asparagus—alone at a large round draped table, four green triangular edges of tablecloth aimed like arrows at the carpeted floor.

Who you lookin at?

She didn't let on. Nobody.

And you, madam?

She sneaked a peek and caught Chitlin Sandwich blowing her a kiss.

Give me dark. Your best.

She wheeled the caged cart and placed the items she needed inside it. She had not been shopping long, when she heard him lewdly cracking his knuckles in the next aisle.

The nexus of speakers blasted out the current chart buster, "Dating Mr. D.," the brainchild of the crunk group Uranium 235.

Saw the death of billions
what could I do?
Sent a message to you punks and bitches
couldn't get through

From her recessed booth she watched dancers shake their hips, little space between the bodies. She shook her head, astonished. How can they dance to this music? Rowdy. She finished her Pepsi. It was hot in her throat, then hot in her stomach. She had been in Salamanders a good hour, having entered it on the lookout, wheeling her eyes about. Her first time. Angela and Niece came here often, but she had always refused to follow. Too loud. Too many young fools. And that dim eye-hurting light. But purpose had drawn her here tonight.

She would bypass Mamma and attack the evil at its source. She had only a dim idea how. But her love for her family would serve as both her dagger and her shield.

These were the last dances before the live music. Sound Productions was scheduled to appear at nine o'clock, ten minutes from now. A small stage had been erected perpendicular to the dance area and parallel to the bar, but the band had yet to appear and set up its equipment.

A black couple—young man, older woman—entered, attached to each other's waists, laughing and keeping time to the music. The woman pointed (with pride? curiosity?) to the stage. The man nodded. They danced their way to the bar, found stools, and ordered drinks. Silver pants, the lady's big horse behind, spread over the bar stool. They sipped their drinks quietly, looking into each other's eyes. The woman set down her glass, flicked its edge with her finger, then leaned over and kissed the man on the tip of his ear. Mouth close, he whispered something. Her soft laugh floated back. She pulled firmly at his tie. Sheila fumbled with her empty glass.

The lady turned her head and looked Sheila full in the face. Her shining eyes seemed to come straight at their target.

Sheila took cover behind her raised hand. Yes. Recognize her anywhere. That's Chitlin Sandwich's mother. The bird-slut.

Sheila lowered her hand and turned her eyes to the dance floor, jammed with waving arms, wiggling bottoms, and shuffling feet. The speakers blared "Tea with Mr. B." by the Sam Hill Roughriders.

> *O woman with a sky in yo thigh*
> *O bitch wit that dip in yo hips*
> *O woman wit yo ass way up high*
> *O bitch wit those dick lips*
> *Call me Mr. B.*
> *Jump my bone bone*
> *Call me Mr. B.*
> *Bone Bone*
> *Come over to my palatial home*
> *Put that high ass way up on my throne*
> *And let me jump them bones*

The floor lit now by clicking light, and the dancers showing up—green, black, green, black—beneath it.

At nine o'clock the music abruptly ceased, and a dapper and nervous announcer took the stage. Look, I'm sorry, folks, but our scheduled band won't be appearing tonight.

The interrupted dancers seemed indifferent.

A traffic jam or something. Sorry. Drinks on the house.

I am the light, I am the load. Skee-dee-skee-dop-ba-du-re-bop-pop-mop-shop-pow! I am the light. I am the load. Skee-dee-slop-pop-be-hop-dop-pow! Born of the cross, birthed on the cross. Died in the bush, dead in the bush. Push. Push. Dead in the bush, red in the push. Gush. Gush. Skee-bop-zop-uh-pow! I am the light, I am the load.

There, in the solitude of her bedroom, she took the phone, the numbers blinking square light in the dark. She put the phone back. Out of her hands now. The simple necessity of faith.

Guess who went to the doctor?

Niece, not again?

Uh-huh. Niece closed her eyes with a wide grin.

So how many will that make? Four?

Five.

You should be ashamed.

Alone on the sofa, in her apartment, Sheila did not share what she was thinking. She had not done so the entire evening.

I already told Frank I ain't never havin no babies. He ain't gon stretch out my coochie. Though married, Angela was fond of a halter and miniskirt and stockingless legs, fond of long strings of pearls that hung from her neck to her knees and a cloche hat that hid her eyebrows.

You can have a Caesarean, Niece said. A bikini cut.

Ain't nobody cuttin me.

They put you under. And they only cut you a little.

No way. Angela shook her head slowly, like a wronged child.

It's simple.

Simple or not simple, ain't nobody takin my boo-boop-a-doop away.

From the couch, Niece kicked her meaty legs in laughter. What about you, Sheila?

Yeah. How come you ain't sayin nothin?

I'm listenin, that's all. Nothing to say.

Bat got yo tongue?

Question. Niece squeezed her face into a serious expression. Do you know how to Mexican-kiss?

Don't ask her that. You know she saved.

I never said that. When did you hear me—

Saved. Saved. Angela clapped her hands and made a song of it.

I'm saved too. Niece tongued her lips.

Many evenings like this. Shades open. A cold wash of stars. Niece had reported her latest fuck while Angela demonstrated the latest dance. Sheila watched them now with flying longing and compassion, for she saw deeper than they could see, deeper, to the indestructible element.

I think Mr. So-and-So at work got a crush on you.

Not on me. You.

Speakin of work, why you ain't finish those files?

I know. I should have.

Well, why didn't you? Gon be hell to pay come Monday morning.

I ain't worried.

You should be.

Sheila pulled her knees to her chin and chest. She sat, silent, and wondering, and staring into the night.

Let's wait a little while longer. (Frank Poor was squat.) We'll be moving along shortly. (No taller than Angela.) No need to rush. (Shorter, perhaps.) We should have a good turnout. (His potbelly—) A thousand people. (—drooping, anchoring him to the earth.) Or more. (Darker than her, black and shiny, like a button.) We did extensive canvassing. (He published his own newspaper, *Make the Rich Pay!*) In fact, did some last-minute canvassing last night. (Taught fire walking on the weekends.) Is this your first?

No, Sheila lied. She had once given to the NAACP. (Or was it the United Negro College Fund?) All told, this was the extent of her political involvement.

Welcome.

Glad to be here.

Fifteen or twenty people formed a broken lopsided sphere on the road. Dressed in athletic gear, as if prepared to run a marathon. Sheila: clothed in the extremity of summer color. Her shoes new and enduring. They patiently waited, conversing, exchanging victories and defeats, tales brought to life again. Sheila listened to it all, speaking when spoken to.

Glad you came out.

Glad you could make it.

She felt her anxiety lift. The touch of harmony.

Play this one by ear. Frank roused the group. Don't think about past experiences. Every leaf is different. Let's remember what we are here to do today.

She joined the line, in military formation. Allowed herself to be propelled forward. Posters waving.

The sky was clear after a morning rain. Beads of water glistened in the rain-washed road. Both sides of the road lined with thickly leaved trees, green and still heavy with rain, their top branches and boughs tangled in the sky.

The people!

United!

Shall never be defeated!

The people!

United!

Shall never be defeated!

Spectators, white and black and otherwise, came out to observe the procession. Laughed and shook their heads as if at some corny circus act.

The hallmark of stupidity. Frank frowned. This nation was founded by men who hid behind barns, and smoked corn silk. And if those lumberjacks—he nodded—are any indication, this is still a country with shit in its boots.

Some ways down the road, Chitlin Sandwich stood in the driveway of Bingo Bob's Car Repair. Chitlin Sandwich. The stiff brooding materiality of youth.

Hey, ain't that the boy who was at the bank?

Yeah. What's his name? Pig Ear Sandwich?

Nawl. Pig Feet.

Fedora pushed back on his head. Stooped, his knees jutting out from under his body. Thick-winged eyebrows that seemed to be drawn down by his open mouth. Heavy eyelids, narrow light in the pupils. His dark (gray? blue?) blazer draped over one crooked arm, while the fingers of the free hand toyed with a gold watch chained—half-loop—to his vest. Sunlight and a diamond tie pin. Sunlight and patent-leather shoes.

Just left of Chitlin Sandwich, a small boy emerged from the shop and climbed atop the white Jaguar fender to get a better view of the procession. Chitlin gave the child a hard look. Grabbed him, lifted him off the fender, kicked him swiftly in the rear, and shoved him back into the shop. That done, he turned and shook his fist at Sheila.

She made no response. She would not give him the satisfaction. Hatch was no longer part of him now. A cool breeze blew from the trees and carried the smell of damp earth and leaves. Set branches moving and covered the road with long flickering shadows.

They crested a hill. Niece dropped behind to seek Man. Sheila found it fitting, elemental. The shrouded road wound off before her, almost lost among the dark trees. Footfalls peppered the silence. Now a new faint noise. She stopped and turned. The white Jaguar descended the hill like a fly down a distended belly. She continued.

She followed the white Jaguar's progress by the roar of its approaching engine. She did not turn to look. She was tough, tougher than expectation.

Air punched her skin. She turned to see Niece rise, rocketlike, into the sky, only to have gravity snatch her rudely back to earth. Before she made impact, her male companion catapulted into the air, a clay pigeon. A scream awakened those standing still in disbelief. Frank tackled Angela into the roadside ditch. Others sought quick refuge in the ditch or farther, in the forest itself. Sheila dropped and rolled, her face buried in tufts of grass. The white Jaguar sped past with a hot gust of wind, spraying dirt and gravel like buckshot into the ditch and leaving behind the smell of hot metal and gasoline. White exhaust fanned and covered the road, phosphorous.

From her place in the ditch, she could no longer see or hear the white Jaguar. Dim screams. Coughs. Gagging. Feet trampling branches and brush. The smoke thinned. Someone gave a shrill warning cry. She watched it all, immediate and remote, tactile, a viewfinder picture. Face rimmed with light, Chitlin Sandwich was bent forward, both hands gripping the steering wheel, eyes almost touching the windshield, teeth tight in a pained smile.

He looked ridiculous. She smothered an impulse to laugh. He sped by, every eye watching, peeled, and crucified.

The Jaguar turned, tires crying. She pushed herself up from the ground. The car came gunning forward, half-slanted in the ditch. She dusted clean her bright summer dress and presented herself to him, memory and substance, mission and will. The car flipped over, rolled down the ditch, and slammed against a tree, then half rolled back up the ditch and fell on its hood, all four wheels topside, like a trained dog's paws. Without pause, red hands edged out of the cab and searched the flattened grass. Hands and body, Chitlin Sandwich crawled from the cab and turned onto his back, still, breathing, opposite the Jaguar's spinning wheels. Sun slanted into the ditch. Chitlin Sandwich. Breathing and bright. The gold watch had broken from gold vest chain. Nowhere in sight. The brim of his fedora directed at the treetops.

Damn, Angela said. Damn. Motherfuck!

The wind carried a blend of dust, exhaust, and blood.

Are they dead?

Crazy bastard.

The motor's hum in her ears, Sheila approached Chitlin Sandwich with fists formed. Like a retractable cup, he rose in circles from the folds of his baggy slacks. Mouth open. Pieces of fractured windshield embedded in his cheek. In one motion, he removed his fedora, his eyes squinting, and swung it in a wide curve. She watched it beyond time, counting the revolutions, aware of the exact moment the sharp brim caught her forehead. More startled than hurt, she sighted what she could of his eyes and gave him her meanest look. He held his hand up for the fedora's return. Caught it. At the ready. Like crude professional wrestlers, Frank and Angela tripped and pinned him to the ditch.

Damn! Motherfuck!

It's okay, Frank said. It's okay.

The Poors were kneeling over Chitlin Sandwich like priests attending the dying. He pedaled his legs like a trapped fly. Mouth gurgling.

Are you all right? Frank both speaking—to Angela? to her?—and holding Chitlin Sandwich in place.

Numb, Sheila touched her forehead. A dab of fresh warm blood on her finger.

Are you okay?

She raised her dress hem—blinded, exposed—and cleaned blood from her forehead.

Are you okay?

She let her dress fall. Yes.

Are you sure?

Yes. I'm fine.

You sure?

Yes.

You know him?

She know him! Angela said. Damn right she know him! She slapped her cloche, with a blast of dust, against her hip.

Conviction, Sheila moved forward in their direction. She did not rush. Her feet could not feel the ground. She seemed to be walking on her ankles. She came to where they knelt. She bent at the waist and picked up Chitlin's fedora. Slapped the dust off her bright summer dress. Reshaped the crown between her fingers.

Stiffened the brim. Empty gestures. Indulgent. Vain. Taunting, perhaps. Challenging. In sum—she judged herself—too little too late, but telling all the same. The Poors seemed to understand. Synchronized, they took to their feet—twins, reflective forms— leaving Chitlin Sandwich unattended. Eyes wide, unbothered by sun, he did not try to rise.

Mississippi Story

It
is my history and
it
is my autobiography
when he sings.
– STERLING PLUMPP, "MISSISSIPPI GRIOT"

The driver takes a quick and cautious glance at me in the rear-view mirror, then returns his calm but vigilant gaze to the highway. Though there's no traffic, he keeps the minivan at a crawl, both hands on the steering wheel, his foot pushing into the hum of the engine. His hair is short and neat, slightly longer than a boot-camp cut. And he is a long-limbed fellow, slim and strong in a long-sleeve cotton shirt and jeans, his skin smooth and bright, milky innocence. "A little town in East Texas. I doubt if you've heard of it."

"No. I don't think I have." I lean forward a bit on the wide seat to hear him better, the joints of my shoulders sore from the plane ride.

"Well, I had never heard of the university back home."

"No?" Dr. Hallard says. The crown of his head rises above the seat cushion in front of me, as bald and pointy as a chess bishop's, a few remnants of hair here and there on his brown wrinkling scalp. He is a professor back East, specializing in Russian history, if I heard him correctly. He rocks about in his seat, trying to make himself comfortable. We're both long in the leg, and the minivan is much smaller than it seems, plush cushions meant to foster the illusion of space. What we both must be thinking: A white boy chauffeuring two black men down a Mississippi highway.

"Not where I'm from. It's kind of isolated. I think my mom was there once. She and my stepdad are driving up next weekend to help me build a shed for one of my professors."

"You keep busy."

"Yes. I've had to since I lost my scholarship."

"Do you still train?"

"I try to find the time."

"You really must. Sixteen feet." Dr. Hallard sighs in astonishment.

"Yes. My best jump."

"Wow."

"There were a couple of other guys back home who could make that jump. One went out to California. One went to New York. He made the U.S. team. I came here and had a good first year, but then I seemed to fall off. I don't know what happened. I was training hard, as hard as I ever had, as hard as I could."

"Yeah, well—" Dr. Hallard shakes his head with the same cheerful resignation he had earlier, on accepting the mishap with his luggage at the airport.

"So, have you been on any digs?" I ask.

"Yes, several. We have quite a few sites right here in Mississippi."

Bleak sunshine. The shuddering windows reveal heavy foliage under an overcast early spring afternoon. Vertical trunks and tightly positioned leaves chart our progress toward the town.

"That's right," Dr. Hallard says. "There are Civil War battle sites throughout this area."

"Several big companies have been constructing strip malls on many of them."

"You don't say."

"Yes."

"Such a shame."

"Quite a few people have been trying to stop them."

"That's good. A railroad used to run right along here." Dr. Hallard points to the grassy roadside beside the opposing lane. I take a long and thorough look. Think I see the ghostly outline of railroad tracks. "They would run their transports up and down here."

"Yes."

"So there were always plenty of raids and acts of sabotage, not to mention actual battles. Oh man. I can't even name all of the battles that happened down here. Let me see." Dr. Hallard taps his fingers on his scalp, sorting through a mental index. "There was Holly Springs, and Corinth. Shiloh, of course. And Tupelo—"

"That's where my family is from," I say.

"Oh yeah?" the driver says. "That's about forty miles east of here."

"Well, not exactly. They're actually from Fulton. Houston."

"So you've been down here before?"

"Used to come all the time when I was a kid to visit my great-aunt. That's been, what, thirty years? Then again, I was here ten, twelve, years ago for her funeral."

"You might want to drive over while you're here."

"Perhaps I will. All this time, I never knew the university was so close to where she lived."

"Less than an hour's drive. Most students hang out and party in Tupelo."

"Rather than Memphis?"

"Yes."

"Why?"

"Tupelo is not quite as far."

"You've been to the battlefield at Tupelo?" Dr. Hallard asks.

"No. We do mostly Indian sites."

"How do you know where to dig? I mean, how do you narrow down a spot?"

"Glad you asked. Let me tell you. We put an infrared camera on a huge helium blimp. Now, this blimp is the size of a basketball court. Bigger. The robotic camera travels along it and pinpoints places where you might find some artifacts. It's quite amazing."

"Wow."

"A blimp, huh?" Me, Hatch, the skeptic.

"Yes."

I think about it, uncertain if I'm impressed. *You have made me glad. At the works of your hands, I sing for joy.*

We ride in silence for a while, tires measuring out time. The highway seems inconsequential in this landscape, like a jackknife that can be folded back into its handle. An occasional car or truck creeping down the road like a steel-and-glass insect. Breaks here and there in the tree-jammed roadside, elbow room for squat houses with compact driveways. (No garages.) Every now and then some ragged suggestion of a farm. Cow or horse or chicken or pond or crop—one fact among many in this terrain of the hidden and the seen.

"What kind of winters do you all get down here?" Dr. Hallard asks.

"Oh, mostly rain. Every once in a while we'll get some snow. Two or three inches hit the ground and everything shuts down."

Many trees at the margins of the highway are stooped over in fascination at whitening earth, twistings of vine and branch like so many whorls on a fingertip.

"Hey, what do you call that stuff?" Dr. Hallard asks.

"Oh, that's kudzu."

"So that's what kudzu looks like."

"Yes. They imported it many many years ago."

"From Japan?"

"I think so. They brought it over to control the spread of rank weed and briar. But it grows like crazy. A month from now it'll cover everything."

I press out the image, all of Mississippi wrapped in a kudzu shawl. Justice.

The road gradually rises to a crest I can't see beyond, then flattens out again. White letters on green metal inform us that the town is two miles ahead.

"You might not know, but tonight is the big night around here. Lots happening."

"Thursday?"

"Right. I don't know why, but Thursday is our Saturday."

"Okay."

"And you should also know that your hotel is a short walk from the town square. Five minutes. Plenty of restaurants there."

"What do you recommend?"

"Benjy's is pretty good. Try their catfish in red-wine sauce."

"Okay. We'll keep it in mind."

Off in the distance I see what appears to be a courthouse with a small yard in front, where a colossal marble pedestal rises some fifty feet above the ground, a bronze soldier mounted there, facing the road to confront all who approach. Closer now, I see a human figure leaning against the pedestal, sharply outlined, in gray coat and black pants, against the stone, this figure shouldering a Confederate flag, black stars patterned into a cross against a dark blue (gray?) background. The rude eyes of witness reveal: a black Confederate soldier.

"What the—? Motherfucker," I say, unmindful of the crude and cutting edges of my words.

"Yes. He's caused some controversy."

I say nothing, for anything I might say seems so much less than what I feel.

The black Confederate is outfitted in a full-length gray coat with a cloaklike attachment, a small, short-brimmed hat—the crown folded over toward his forehead like a scorpion's stinger—and black jeans and black gym shoes. His flag is attached to a pole no thicker than a broom handle, certainly not military standard or military-issue. An old rusty Boy Scout canteen crosses his chest and waist. His skin is so dark that his fingernails glow like tracer bullets.

"Next month we will be voting on a referendum to remove the flag from the state capitol and all state buildings." The driver jerks his head toward the Confederate. "He wants them to keep it up."

"What?"

"Now I've seen it all," Dr. Hallard says.

"Some kind of joke?" I ask.

"I don't know. All I can say for sure is that he's caused quite a bit of controversy."

The driver circles the square, circles the courthouse, circles the bronze statue. I can't chance a good view of the reb's face, but he moves his head in our direction, peeps us, and raises the flag higher. Somehow, I feel that we are on display, the three of us in the minivan like some rare species behind glass.

Moments later, we exit the minivan in the hotel's driveway. I search through my wallet, slide free a five, the biggest tip I can spare, a full two dollars more than what I would normally give.

The town is fighting to keep Applebee's, Banana Republic, Old Navy, Wal-Mart, and Circuit City out of the courthouse square, where uniform two-story brick-and-wood buildings with verandas perched on ten-foot-high posts house expensive shops and services, bars and boutiques, restaurants and cafés. On Friday nights, book clubs cram into the confined spaces of these shops. The town prides itself on being a literary community and boasts more reading groups than any other municipality in Mississippi. Homes in the immediate radius of the square—rehabbed antebellum structures and their modern imitations—hold the market at a million dollars or more per property. A national magazine recently honored the town with a high distinction, calling it the third-best retirement community in America.

In a small garden left of the entryway to the redbrick cement-lined library, a bronze statue of F. dressed in hat, suit, and tie is seated at the far end of a glazed (green gray) park bench, both taller and larger than F. actually was in life. His legs are crossed at the knees, with his left hand resting on them, right arm across the top of the bench back, so that he is seated at an angle, turned slighty toward the viewer, smoking pipe in (right) hand—a man both relaxed and dignified, inviting the viewer to sit down and join him. Dull metal clothing and skin are set against a fresh bright bed of red tulips and varicolored perennials, directly behind him. A small slim-trunked tree is planted ninety degrees to his right, the leaves either the palest of green or dried to a brown autumn tint and crumpled. And bronze and bench are positioned in the left extremity of a mosaic arc, alternating bands of rectangular red stone and curved green slab.

I continue on to the square's center, where a small group of white reporters have flocked around the black Confederate, cameras swooping about, pens pecking words onto their notepads, microphones perched in air. From the tone of his voice, I can tell that he is taking a firm stand on the issues, gesturing with emphasis and keeping tabs with his fingers. I take a moment to lock his physical details into memory. The small gray hat has a thin black belt across the front, a tiny gold buckle dead center above the short black visor. With its folded-over crown, the hat reminds me of an old ice bag. (My aunt would unscrew the lid, drop a few perfectly square cubes into the pouch, twist the lid tight, then place the pouch, cold and hard, on a lump.) The ice-bag reb is a man in his early to mid thirties with pronounced cheekbones that form a thick V under each deep-set eye, a nose so compact and modest you might overlook it, and lips no larger than a nickel. He gives me an offhand glance. The camera finds him. He actually stops talking and poses for me, left foot on the curb, left hand positioned on left knee, eyes looking slightly to his right—off camera—flag across his right shoulder. The flag hand also holds a small black disk, a portable CD player, the headphones draped about his red-shirted neck. The shutter moves and emblazons him in celluloid. His damn-fool twin distant and small on a light-catching strip.

Bent at the waist, a man my age and of my build prepares to enter his compact Japanese car. He looks up, sees me, and straightens himself, keys in hand. "How are you?"

"Fine. How about you?"

"Never been better." He approaches me. "Hey, can I ask you something?"

"Sure." I'm expecting some mundane question about weather or directions.

"Did you talk to that guy?"

"Not really."

"Did you hear what he was saying?"

"I really wasn't listening. I mean, I wasn't even trying to hear what he had to say. I figured he was crazy, that's all."

"He ain't crazy. No, sir. I knew that guy way back in high school. He may be tricky. Ain't crazy, though. He been tellin all these reporters that he's got a wife over in London and a brother in Germany and that he's got a degree from this college and a plaque from this organization. All kinds of stuff. He's got a whole lotta them supporting him."

"Uh-huh. So you think he fakin it? Hustlin them?"

"I'll put it to you like this. He don't care nothin bout no white folks."

From the *Daily*:
The university police department states the following incidents have been reported between Wednesday, March 14, and Tuesday, March 20:

Suspicious Persons
Monday, March 19, 3:31 p.m.,
UPD received a report of a suspicious person in the J. D.
Williams Library. The person was described as a black
male, no facial hair, and in his mid 20s. Negative contact
was made with the person by UPD.

Friday, March 16, 9:52 a.m.,
UPD received a report of a suspicious person in the lobby
area of Carrier Hall. He was described as a black male,
approximately 5'6"–5'7" tall, 160–175 lb, short hair, clean
shaven, and dark complexion. He entered an office, where
he asked to use the phone and also asked if there was any
food in the building.

Dr. Hallard and I are the first guests to arrive for the cocktail party at an antebellum mansion, a white two-story structure with six green slat-backed wooden rocking chairs positioned across a long wide porch.

"Isn't this something?" he says.

"True that. Sure we should go in? We might not get out."

He laughs.

We enter the house and go right to the bar, discreet, taking little notice of our grand surroundings. Dr. Hallard is taller than I am, and I have come to learn that he is a jocular man. He tells me how much he likes my work, that I'm the real deal, how he can't wait to read more.

"Well," I say, "I learned everything I know from you." I give him a playful slap on his blazer-covered back. I've never read him.

"Oh no." He laughs. "I'm just a historian trying my hand at new things in my old age."

"That's where we're alike. I try my hand too."

A sharply dressed middle-aged woman approaches us. She has a long face and a protruding mouth like a sea horse's. "Hi, I'm Mrs. Jason. I'm with the university."

"Glad to meet you."

"You're—"

"Yes. And this is Dr. William Hallard."

"Of course, I recognized you both. So glad you could join us."

"Glad to be here."

"You folks enjoying yourselves?"

"Most definitely."

"Good."

"This is some house."

"Have you had a look around?"

"No."

"Please do."

I set off in one direction, and Dr. Hallard sets off in another. I wander through odd-shaped rooms that open one out into another. Let my gaze wander over gaudy Victorian settees and sofas, four-footed mahogany bookcases with scrolled cupboard doors, cylinder-topped bureaus on bow-legs and bun feet, peg-calved corner tables, inlaid *bonheurs du jour*, etched display cabinets, heavy curtains like mounds of hardened lava, narrow-shouldered grandfather clocks like genetically altered men. Every inch of the papered walls blocked with paintings—equestrians, seascapes, landscapes, and portraits—tree, sail, saddle, and cheek textured in age-thickened curls of oil.

The house quickly fills. People casual in conversation. Tilted heads and raised glances. Tinkling ice. Quiet sips. I make many introductions, names and professional descriptions that I quickly forget. I make my way back to the bar, where the bartender is hard at work, his hands circling a small table with a neat arrangement of tonic and seltzer water, vodka and soda, wine and whiskey, lime and lemon. He wears a white shirt, black bowtie crossed at the throat, and black slacks, and speaks in a high light cadence, like a rock skipping over water. He hands me my gin and tonic in a plastic cup.

"Would you know the story behind this house?" I take a sip. Just right. Take another sip.

"Yes. It's a miracle it's still standing. They burned everything else." His face reveals no emotion. Shark gaze, eyes black and blank. "It was owned by a doctor who treated both sides during the war."

"I see."

"The university purchased it a few years ago."

"Well, thanks for enlightening me."

"My pleasure. Like another?"

"Yes." I watch him prepare the drink, words stirring inside. I take my drink and hurry off to the dining room. Guests gathered around a cloth-covered mahogany table crowded with plates, pots, and utensils. Some fishy substance—life feeds on life—in rectangular pans kept warm by flaming canned heat. Dinner rolls like bare baby butts cradled in a wicker basket. Salad growing in glass bowls. Dressed like checkerboard squares—white shirt, black pants, white apron, black shoes—bustling attendants enter and exit the room, trays at the ready.

"Is that crayfish?" I ask one of them.

"Crawfish," she says.

"Okay. That's how we say it where I'm from."

"And where's that?"

I tell her.

"I have family up north."

"Do you."

"Enjoy your food."

"I will."

I eat till I am stuffed. Clean my hands on a cloth napkin and toss it on a waiter's shouldered platter. Then I travel down a long hall—with a polished floor like a wooden runway—that leads to the roped-off upper story, oak banister gleaming like a wet tongue. I take a seat on the carpeted stairway, red rope inches above my head. I down my drink, neck craned back and plastic cup covering my mouth, muzzlelike. Sight along liquored edge and see a woman smiling down at me. A saloned blond in her early to mid forties, pure East Coast elegance in a black party dress with perfectly matched jewelry. Her skin is puffy, rebellious, refuses to stay flat.

"Did you try the crawfish?"

I lower my cup. "Yes. Delicious."

"Do say. Dessert should be ready soon."

"I can't wait."

"So, how do you like our town?"

"Fine, so far."

"Your first time here?"

"Yes. Well, not exactly. My folks come from these parts. Houston."

"Oh, that's only about forty miles east of here."

"So I've been told. I used to visit my great-aunt every summer when I was a kid."

"Well, enjoy your stay."

"I plan to."

"I think you'll find the people in town are more than friendly. They'll go out of their way to help you. Anything you need, just ask."

"I will."

"And, you know, before you leave, you should go down to Benjy's and try their shrimp-and-grits dinner. It's an absolute delicacy."

"I will."

I make my way back to the bar and discover Dr. Hallard, drink in hand, keeping the interest of a circle of listeners. (Perhaps he will hold them seven nights with seven hundred tales.) I follow the path of duty to the sitting room, where a squadron of eaters and talkers are sprawled about in high-backed armchairs. I talk to this person and that but soon run out of things to say. Conversation congeals into polite patterns. Attentive gazes and curious glances recede into fatigue or boredom. Faces go lax from alcohol. I scan the room for fresh skin. Survey the mansion one last time. Have another drink or two. End up back where I started. Voices pelt me, bang and run rough. I could attack. I could trot like a bull through every room of this fucking mansion, charge my enemies head-on, bumping and butting those who refused to give way. Stomp down ugly. Instead, I escape to the porch and scoot into a rocking chair. I am tiny inside it, a baby in a high seat. Notice a huge oak just left of the house as wide as three men. Stare out at the road, a dark screen of trees behind it. And I listen. Insects humming like incoming missiles.

I rise from the chair and set out for the hotel. The night rises and falls before me, trees shimmering in the lamped dark. Hot blots of light where moths and gnats and winged anonymous others stick and burn, their wings like flaming shrouds. I can hear their panic. If I am attentive, if I incline my ear, these woods will tell me great secrets.

"In mythical geography, sacred space is essentially *real space*, for . . . in the archaic world the myth alone is real. It tells of manifestations of the only indubitable reality—the *sacred*."

My oldest cousin and I catch a flight to Memphis, rent a car at the airport, and find a cheap motel just outside of Fulton owned and operated by Indians from India. We sit in silence, he on his bed and I on mine, staring down at the dark lake of floor between us, hoping to draw up memories from forgotten deeps. The next day we help lower our aunt's coffin into a freshly dug grave, fist by fist. I feel the rope tug and pull, the red dirt shift under my feet, feel myself being yanked forward, snatched down into the open box of earth.

"Wasn't that in Jackson?" The receiver tight against my ear, wedged between my shoulder and cheek.

"No," my mother says. "Tupelo."

"Tupelo?"

"Yes."

I am watching a watercolored landscape, broad pastures and fields rimmed by a cheap metal frame.

"The Klan headquarters was right there downtown. I think it still is. The only place in the world where I've ever seen one."

"That's what I was wondering." I unfold a map of Mississippi and spread it across the bed. "Because somebody at the party said that Jackson is south of here. And all this time I thought we took the bus from Memphis through Jackson to Tupelo."

"No way."

"Now I know."

All this time, these many years, I've had the geography wrong. I've told people that my family comes from the delta. But the delta is a five- or six-hour drive south of here. I'm starting to learn that Mississippi is larger than I had imagined. Its boundaries have slowly grown since I was a child. The state busting its seams, moving out into space, ragged at its edges like an ink blot on paper.

"What do they have scheduled for tomorrow?"

"Nothing important. In fact, I don't plan to attend any of the morning events."

"Won't they be expecting you?"

"They might be. I plan on having a look at the F. estate. It's supposed to be a short walk from here."

"Do you think that's a good idea?"

"I don't believe they'll—"

"I wouldn't do too much walking around down there, if I were you."

In one corner of the cemetery, the F. family plot is surrounded by a low concrete wall with the family name chiseled on limestone carved in the form of a columned Greek arch, three to four feet in height. F. and his wife are buried inside parallel tombs, their place of final resting memorialized by two marble plates, each six feet in length and four in width, surfaces almost metallic in the sun. Trees cast a black mass of shadow over the graves, a jutting peninsula in the shape of a black branch, jagged leaves like toothy-edged archipelagos. I'd heard that the cemetery keeps a bottle of Jack Daniel's whiskey at the plot for visitors so that they can take a sip in F.'s honor, as a libation of sorts. I see the remnants of a bottle, a handful of knuckle-sized chunks of glass and square fragments with weather-faded labels. F.'s dog has earned burial rights in a parallel plot:

> *E.T.*
>
> *AN OLD*
> *FAMILY*
> *FRIEND*
> *WHO CAME*
>   *HOME*
> *TO REST*
> *WITH US*

I set the camera's self-timer and kneel beside the Greek arch.

I had hoped to visit the Heritage Museum, which has a collection of more than fifty battle flags, but then I learn that the flags are too fragile to be displayed. I turn down an invitation to attend church and on aimless feet head out of town on one of the main roads. A cat lies sprawled in a ditch, its pink tongue curling stiffly to the ground, stretched like bubble gum. Just a ways up, a priest stands on the wide cement walk outside his church—a modern structure with a sleek frame, airy doors and windows, a roof boldly tinted like the blood of Sacrament, and a cross carved with an artist's keen and distinctive touch—and fellowships with wafer-skinned members of his parish. Smiling, talking, laughing, shaking hands, patting backs, kissing babies, and pinching cheeks. His skin is a shade or two lighter than his black cloak. (Black absorbs everything, even cast-off sin.) He seems much older than his parishioners, well-groomed go-getters in their twenties and thirties who sport designer clothes and drive luxury cars. (The parking lot jammed full.) He is balding, the last of his hair putting up a good fight, a tight black band clinging to the back and sides of his head, a bat with wings clamped. His jaw is lined and twisted, head screwed into his white collar. (White repels. May starched collar keep the devil away from soft throat.) And the expression on his face is by turns sympathetic, pensive, and joyful. In ear distance, I can just make out the words "We can kneel down together or alone anytime, anywhere, and ask for God's help."

I want to say something to knock the wind out of him. Does he whiff toe jam at the foot of the cross? Does Lazarus have night-mares about the shunned grave? I bite my tongue. Men are made from the earth and shall return to it. No match for Holy Ghost power.

I concentrate on my footwork, leather rhythm. (During the Civil War, popular consciousness developed a theory to explain the tremendous endurance of men in battle. Called the theory of the conversion of force, it postulated that every shock was absorbed into the body and stored in the form of energy.) Clean-framed homes with aluminum siding give way to weeded lots spotted with rusty metal milk cans like hollowed-out bombshells, hitching posts covered in ghostly mold, shriveled-up sheds sinking into the earth. Long-abandoned antebellum dwellings decaying there, wood in-dented with the tooth marks of storms. Lumber exploding out at wild angles. Rooms sheared away. Porch and plank constricted in snakelike brambles. Unhinged trellises curling away from structure like suspended high-wire acrobats. Architectural achievements re-duced to antiquated puzzles of oak and timber.

Sun straggles—yellow, then red—across the sky. Trees hold their formation, kudzu laced through trunks and leaves. At one point I must appear lost, a dark fugitive, because a white man pulls his car over to the graveled shoulder, steps out of it, and asks if I need assistance. No, I tell him. He offers me a ride. I like to walk, I tell him.

Well, you have a good day, now.

The same to you.

A mile or two later, an old black man comes rolling down the road on a golf cart, shouting pronouncements through a bullhorn. I later discover that he is the only black mayor in the county. He quiets down for a moment to greet me. Rolls on. A welcome introduction to geographical extremes, communities dotting the forest like dice flung and let be. Mississippi still the poorest state in the Union, although black people have owned land in this part of the state since the days immediately following the war's end. No shotgun shacks here. Native sons and daughters live in six-bedroom trailer homes with working fireplaces and bubbling Jacuzzis.

Nothing like my aunt's home in Fulton—Mississippi continually spoils my recollection of things—a range house with one door opening into her living room and out onto the front lawn, and a second door, a side exit-entrance, taking you through the kitchen to a cement overhang and cement patio paved all the way down to the noisy gravel driveway. She would dress in men's overalls and rubber boots and go hunt for heavy watermelons—yellow meat inside—that grew wild behind her house in the wooded decline that everyone called "the snake pit."

Sweat spills, a river inside me. My feet cramped, confined in shoes too stubborn to break. Murder, each step. Hot water rising in my chest, I draw in fire, expel ash. Drop down in roadside dirt. Shut my eyes and try to picture my aunt's face.

That night, in my hotel room, I attempt to write her a letter. Words reverberate in the air like hummingbirds. I can see it all taking shape. (Sound the trumpets.) I lie back on the bed, hands cupped behind my neck, dirty shoes extended over mattress edge. I stare at the white ceiling until I can see through to the bone, down to the collagen, reflective substance that reveals.

At the complimentary breakfast buffet, I nurse a cup of gritty coffee and munch on wedges of cool watermelon while Dr. Hallard, between hearty crunches of toast and bacon and forkfuls of scrambled eggs, gives me the lowdown on a story he read in the morning paper. Tongue red with strawberry jam, he tells me about a black woman in some remote Florida town who draped her baby's carriage in the Confederate flag, then camped out before the courthouse. Handcuffed, she is reported to have said, "It's our history too."

I leave the hotel to a cyclone of embraces. Promises to call or write. Visit. At the airport, I find a cool seat in a wedge of shadow and wait for the plane to begin boarding. Dressed in identical outfits (white blouse, red vest, and black skirt), three ticket agents—a white woman sandwiched between two black women—power walk down the long lobby, elbows working frantically like clipped bird wings, chattering through labored breaths. The woman closest to me carries a half-empty bottle of water that the three must be sharing. *All of us are being transformed into the same image, from one degree of glory to another.* They reach the lobby's end, then circle back the way they came. Five minutes later, they reach the lobby's end and circle back.

"They kept giving me a hard time. Then somehow it came out that I was a student at the university. You should have seen the looks on their faces. They had a truck bring it all the way from Memphis to Mississippi and everything. Even gave me a discount."

"Wow."

"People love that school down here."

"The Harvard of the South."

"I'd rather be at Harvard."

"So, did they throw in a free wadermeln?"

"'Watermelon.' I'm going to break you out of your country ways."

"Who's country? I'm not country. You country."

"I'm not country."

"You the one from Memphis."

"Everybody from Memphis is not country."

"Okay. Whatever you say."

"Everybody down here doesn't talk like you."

"That's my Mississippi roots."

"Don't blame it on Mississippi."

"You've made your point."

"So you should start—"

"I need to ask you a favor."

"What?"

"A favor. That's the main reason I called. Think you could drive over to Fulton and take a few photographs of my aunt's house?"

"Fulton? I don't know anything about Fulton."

"Didn't say you did. But it's not that far from you. You must know somebody who knows."

"Perhaps."

"Come on."

"How do you even know the house is still there?"

"It might not be."

Several years ago, fish farmers brought Asian carp to the Mississippi River to harvest them after flooding had severely reduced the number of catfish and other local species. On their own these carp learned to defy their environment. They jump out of the water, three to four feet into the air, like dolphins and bang into the side of casino ships or fall onto the hook- and worm-crowded decks of low-sided boats. These carp weigh six pounds now but will weigh twenty pounds a year from now. Of course, there is no market for fish that fly.

It Shall Be Again

You can tear a building down
But you can't erase a memory.
– LIVING COLOUR

Pennies rained from heaven in thick dirty color. Penny rain, ringing against parked cars, breaking windshields and windows, bouncing off concrete, rolling into sewers, spinning like plates. Sweat and work: Hatch played off-the-wall with a rubber ball against the ugly ribs of an old school building. In one motion, he caught the ball and shoved it deep into his pants pocket. He stood in the vacant lot and watched the world pass.

Open, coons chased pennies with brown grocery bags, coins cutting through. Coons abandoned their places in the lottery line and pulled at the sky with raised fists. Pennies spilled from windows and doorways. Coons fell from roofs with outstretched hands. Stud coons used they asshole for a purse, and bitch coons they pussy. Disbelief—awe—kept some rooted in shock. Not Boo. He plunged squarely into the business, clawing up coins like a bear fish. *Stupid coon*, Hatch thought. Never knew how stupid till now. Boo lived in a basement dark, damp, and smelly like a ship's hold. Once a week Hatch boarded the ship—Ai, mate! Let's take to the seas, he teased. Hol de win, hol de win, hol de win. Don't let it blow—

and tutored Boo in math and reading. Boo savored the sweetness of strength and gaffled his peers for their lunch money. Every day he ate two big-ass slices of white bread (Hatch liked wheat), two lumps of mayonnaise (Hatch liked Miracle Whip), and two long rolls of pennies. To curry favor and keep Boo from beating his ass, Hatch had taught him this penny sandwich. Save for the future, he said. You'll always have something in your stomach.

Save. He bagged and transported groceries for Hi-Lo Foods. Seven, he earned a third of a man's salary but could outthink anybody thirty times his size and thirty-three times his age.

Boo was at the other end of the vacant lot, open mouth aimed at the sky. He swallowed his fill of pennies, full to the stitches like the Pillsbury Doughboy, then headed home, slow and heavy. Vomiting pennies, shitting pennies, pissing copper.

Old ladies ran out the stained-glass doors of the Ambassadors for Church of God in Christ, the Elder Milton Oliver, pastor. (They sat on pews all day, hoping to levitate the building with their waving fans.)

If coons are this worked up, surely the white folks downtown must be really showing out. Hell, I ain't gon chase no pennies. Be rich someday. His confidence was grounded in a structural vision. Heaven, Incorporated. Try Jesus—You'll Like Him. Dial 1-800-OMYLORD and talk to Jesus directly. (Free blessing with every call!) Five hundred dollars will buy you a train ticket to heaven. One-time offer. Fifty dollars for your key to the kingdom (twenty-four-karet gold). One-hundred-dollar yearly membership for the Angel Club. (Purchase your wings first! Available in nylon, satin, and silk. White or off-white.) Twenty-five dollars to reserve your bed in the upper room. He would build big-ass churches the size of football stadiums, rising on every street, on every corner, in every neighborhood. Churches as big as cities rising above county, state, and country. Hell, I might even put some on the moon. Hire me the best preachers: Sterling Pickens of the First Baptist

Multimedia Church, Rich "Ducats" Allen (Lay de foundation; build a home in dat rock; lift up this hammer; Gawd'll put you to work), Stallion Blade (It ain't bout the salary, it's all bout reality). Five-dollar cover charge or ten-thousand-dollar yearly membership. Bucket-deep collection plates. Yes, I'm gon be all money someday. Head as flat as a dime. Diamond fingernails. Jeweled three-ton suit. Gold cane, fat like an elephant's dick. Clockin dollars.

Knuckles, pennies punched through faces. Dragon's teeth, chewed-up hands and feet. Sprayed brownstones clean. Leveled new houses and coppered old ones with squat layered covering like the shells of armored trucks.

In a burst of thunder (God's fart), the sky closed.

The once hollow-cheeked were now frog-jawed with pennies. Green eyes were greener. Coons cradled coins in arms like children. (One bitch coon rocked her bundle back and forth.) The dark streets glowed copper paths. And under the streetlights, yellow blue red things, twitching or still. Some dressed, some naked. Some with calm faces, others with wide looks of terror.

Maybe the next time it will rain nickels, dimes, quarters, half-dollars, and round dollars. Maybe the sky will pave streets in silver. Level steel skyscrapers and mold them into tracks. Forge the entire city into a massive silver railroad. Guess who gon be the conductor? Choo choo! Whistling and weaving.

No sooner had he thought this, when it began to rain again.

He knew all the names for his people and recited them. Chocolate drops, coons, niggers, niggas, nigras, jungle bunnies, moolies, tar babies, sambos, spooks, spades, spear chuckers, darkies, geechies, coloreds, negroes, Negroes, blacks, Blacks, Afro-Americans, African Americans. Falling like bad dancers. Flopping like fish.

JEFFERY RENARD ALLEN is the author of two collections of poetry, *Stellar Places* (Moyer Bell, 2007) and *Harbors and Spirits* (Moyer Bell, 1999), and of the widely celebrated and influential novel, *Rails Under My Back* (Farrar, Straus and Giroux, 2000), which won the *Chicago Tribune*'s Heartland Prize for Fiction. His other awards include a Whiting Writer's Award, the Chicago Public Library's Twenty-first Century Award, a Recognition for Pioneering Achievements in Fiction from the African American Literature and Culture Association, a support grant from Creative Capital, and the 2003 Charles Angoff award for fiction from *The Literary Review*. He has been at fellow at the Dorothy and Lewis B. Cullman Center for Scholars and Writers at the New York Public Library, a John Farrar Fellow in Fiction at the Bread Loaf Writers' Conference, and a Walter E. Dakins Fellow in Fiction at the Sewanee Writers' Conference.

His essays, reviews, fiction, and poetry have appeared in numerous publications, including the *Chicago Tribune, Poets & Writers, Triquarterly, Ploughshares, Bomb, Hambone, The Antioch Review, StoryQuarterly, African Voices, African American Review, Callaloo, Arkansas Review, Black Renaissance Noire*, and *XCP: Cross Cultural Poetics*. His work has also appeared in several anthologies, including *110 Stories: New York Writes after September 11, Rainbow Darkness: An Anthology of African American Poetry, Chicago Noir*, and *Homeground: Language for an American Landscape*.

Born in Chicago, he holds a Ph.D. in English (Creative Writing) from the University of Illinois at Chicago and is an instructor in the graduate writing program at New School University. He has also taught for Cave Canem, for the Summer Literary Seminars program in St. Petersburg, Russia, for Kwani in Nairobi, Kenya, and in the writing program at Columbia University. He is the founder and executive director of the Pan African Literary Forum, an international literary organization that serves and aids writers and that holds an annual writers' conference. Allen lives in Far Rockaway, Queens.

The text of *Holding Pattern* has been set in Adobe Jenson Pro, a typeface drawn by Robert Slimbach and based on late-fifteenth-century types by the printer Nicolas Jenson. Book design by Ann Sudmeier. Composition by BookMobile Design and Publishing Services, Minneapolis, Minnesota. Manufactured by Versa Press on acid-free paper.